Dangerous Dance

Matt pulled her gently against him as the song built to its soulful crescendo, and felt the most incredible sense of rightness and peace. It felt so good, it ached inside him. He brushed his lips against Sarah's temple, his breath stirring the baby-fine tendrils of hair that curled there like wisps of silk.

As the last strains of the melody drifted away Sarah stepped back and looked up at him, her eyes so dark a blue, they looked the color of pansies. She stared up at him for a long moment, saying nothing, her expression carefully blank.

"Sarah." He didn't know what he meant to say. All that came out was her name as soft as a secret.

"I . . . I'd best say good night," she whispered, backing slowly away from him.

He stayed where he was, watching her go, saying nothing. Then she was in the comforting dark of the hall. She curbed the urge to run. By the time she got to the stairs, she stopped altogether, her hands clutching the polished oak newel post.

"Oh, dear heaven," she whispered, her voice trembling with emotion. "Please don't let this happen. Please don't let me fall in love with him."

But as she climbed the stairs to her room, she had the terrible feeling it was already too late for prayers.

BANTAM BOOKS BY TAMI HOAG

Sarah's Sin

Tami Hoag

BANTAM BOOKS
NEW YORK • TORONTO • LONDON • SYDNEY • AUCKLAND

SARAH'S SIN

A Bantam Book

PUBLISHING HISTORY

Bantam Loveswept edition published July 1991
Bantam paperback edition / December 1992

ISBN 0-553-56050-6

Published simultaneously in the United States and Canada

Bantam Books are published by Bantam Books, a division of Random
House, Inc. Its trademark, consisting of the words "Bantam Books" and the
portrayal of a rooster, is Registered in U.S. Patent and Trademark Office and
in other countries. Marca Registrada. Bantam Books, 1540 Broadway, New
York, New York 10036.

PRINTED IN THE UNITED STATES OF AMERICA

OPM   29   28   27   26   25   24   23   22

AUTHOR'S NOTE

While the town of Jesse, Minnesota, is purely a figment of my own overactive imagination, there is indeed a fair-sized Amish population in Minnesota's southeastern corner based around the towns of Harmony and Canton. It is in this area that I grew up.

The influx of Amish did not come until the mid-seventies, but they are now a firmly established community and have played a vital role in the area's economic recovery from the agricultural depression of the early eighties by attracting tourists to this very lovely part of the state.

So if you ever have the yearning for rolling countryside and the sound of buggy wheels clattering along the shoulder of the road, for the slower pace of small-town life and a place where everybody knows everybody else by name, I've got just the place for you.

1

He looked dead.

Sarah Troyer sat beside the bed, her eyes wide and unblinking as she stared at the man whose care she had been charged with. He lay motionless, only his head visible above the black-and-purple quilt that covered the bed. He was perhaps thirty-two or thirty-three, but he seemed older in his unconscious state. Even in the amber glow of the bedside lamp, his skin was the color of parchment. His left eye was swollen along the brow and discolored like a peach gone bad. A neat line of stitches embroidered his chin at an angle. In spite of his injuries, his face was strong and handsome, with a high, broad forehead and bold black brows, a stubborn-looking chin and a wide, well-defined mouth that kept drawing her gaze like a magnet.

"Melanie, Melanie," he mumbled, a hint of a smile turning up the corners of his mouth. "Kiss me where it hurts."

A warm sensation wriggled through Sarah from the top of her head down, prickling her scalp beneath the fine white mesh fabric of her

Amish *kapp* and curling her toes in her sensible black shoes. It wasn't just fear and it wasn't just guilt, this feeling. It was excitement. For once in her quiet, sheltered life she was going to have an adventure.

Automatically her mind spun out the words like a gossamer thread to weave a story with. . . . *Once upon a time* . . .

"Oh, man, I've died and gone to *Little House on the Prairie*."

At the sound of the masculine voice Sarah jerked awake, her body snapping to attention faster than her foggy mind. The jolt of all her muscles coming to life at once sent her shooting off the edge of her chair. She landed with a thud, her bottom connecting solidly with the hard braided oval rug beside the bed.

While the idea of helping a lovely lady up appealed to him enormously, Matt Thorne didn't move an inch. He couldn't; he ached in so many places, the electrical impulses his brain sent to his muscles kept shorting out en route. Bleary-eyed, he merely stared at the feminine face now peering up at him over the edge of the bed.

Her quick trip to the floor had left visible only the top of her head, two enormous dark blue eyes, and an impudent tip-tilted nose. Though her hair was mostly covered, he could see that it was thick and rich brown. She wore it up but whisper-wisps escaped their bonds to curl around the edges of her face.

She had on an old-fashioned kind of nurse's uniform he'd never seen before—a blue dress with a black apron over it and a small white cap that seemed to have been fashioned out of stiff gauze. She looked like a student nurse from some religious college for virtuous young women. Beguiling innocence radiated from those fathomless blue eyes. There was an untouched quality about the ripe curve of her cheek. A virgin nurse. Not a bad fantasy, Matt decided, mustering a ghost of his notorious smile.

"Isn't this a little above and beyond the call of duty?" he asked, his voice still rough with sleep. "Or is vigil-keeping a speciality at Our Lady of Guileless Chastity School for Girls?"

The blue eyes blinked at him, then went on staring. A shy young thing. Somewhere beneath the layers of bruises and teeth-grinding pain, Matt's sixth sense stirred to life. It was his personal built-in woman-o-meter, a kind of finely tuned radar that alerted him to all the subtle nuances of the women around him. It was in part what had made him a legend in the corridors of County General. It homed in now on the delightful young lady peering over the edge of the bed at him like a cornered mouse waiting for the house tomcat to pounce.

"You can relax, Blue Eyes," he murmured, shifting a little on the bed and wincing as an invisible knife of pain slipped between his cracked ribs. "I'm in no condition to endanger your standing with the good sisters of your order."

Sarah felt a guilty flush creep into her cheeks. He thought she was a nun, but she doubted nuns let their hearts go racing at the sight of eyes as dark and sparkling as a starlit night. She doubted nuns let their stomachs flip-flop at the sound of a man's voice.

She had meant to sit in the chair only a moment or two, but she'd dozed off and her cursedly vivid imagination had taken the fragile thread of the story she'd begun and whipped it into a full-blown tapestry of a dream wherein she had nursed Matt Thorne back from death's door and he had then swept her away on a romantic whirlwind tour of the world.

And he thought she was a nun. So much for her fantasy. The practical half of her wondered why she persisted in indulging in romantic daydreams anyway. They were not at all the sort of thing she had been raised to think about or expect. An Amish woman's life was one of servitude to God and her family. Tours of the world were well beyond her experience or expectation, so what was the point in dreaming about them? Of course, the insatiable, incorrigible dreamer in her had hidden behind her cowardice and had no answer with which to soothe her conscience. With a fatalistic sigh she pushed herself to her feet and dusted off her skirts.

"I am not a nun, Matt Thorne," she said, irritated more by her own disappointment in herself than by his mistake.

Her voice was soft and husky, accented with the flavor of a German dialect that must be her first language. Matt liked the way it sounded—homespun and warm. He managed to spread another of those sweet melting smiles across his face. "There's a welcome piece of news."

Sarah's heart skipped. His voice was little more than a whisper, but it was strong and as warm and textured as a woolen blanket. She imagined she could feel it drift from his mouth and wrap around her. Heat flared under her skin. She took a resolute step back from the edge of the bed and folded her hands primly in front of her.

"I am Amish," she stated in the way a costumed guide at some living history theme park might.

"Amish," Matt repeated absently, taking another look at her.

He couldn't shake the feeling that she looked untouched, unspoiled, from the top of her little white cap to the tips of her black shoes. She looked young—maybe eighteen or nineteen.

She wore no makeup, no jewelry, just the costume of her people and a look of wide-eyed innocence that was touching his heart in all its most tender places. Her dress was long-sleeved and hung nearly to her ankles. Any womanly curves it might have inadvertently revealed were covered by her apron. She looked like a vision out of the last century, and he wondered if he was indeed conscious or just having a very bizarre dream. What was an Amish woman doing beside his bed?

A little more of the drug-induced mist cleared from his mind, and for the first time since waking up he took a look at his surroundings. The room was vaguely familiar, furnished with antiques, the wallpaper a dark blue background with a riot of tiny flowers strewn over it. The place smelled pleasantly of lemon oil and potpourri. He dredged up a fragment of memory about leaving the hospital—not as he had left it nearly every day for the last six years, as head honcho of County General's emergency room, but on the other side of the wheelchair, as a patient. That seemed like weeks ago, even though he doubted it had been a day since he'd been released. Nothing like a few painkillers to warp a man's sense of time.

"Ingrid," he mumbled. "Ingrid brought me here. Jessup, Justice, J-something."

"Jesse."

His smile was automatic, a conditioned response to the stimulus of a woman's voice. It wasn't full voltage, but even at half power it was usually effective in weakening feminine defenses. "I'm pleased to meet you, Jesse," he said in a voice like silk.

Sarah felt her knees go soft, and a brief fluttering of panic beat in the base of her throat like a butterfly's wings. She had never had this kind of reaction to a man before, not even to her late husband. She had read about it, but had decided it was something only English women experienced. She had envied them the excitement, but now that she was feeling it firsthand, she didn't much care for the sensation.

Taking a deep breath, she steeled herself against Matt Thorne's charm and scowled at him. "I'm not Jesse. The town is Jesse. My name is Sarah Troyer."

"Sarah," Matt said and sighed dramatically, letting his head roll across his pillow. "That's even better," he said, glancing sideways at her. "Sarah is a lovely name."

"So is Melanie," she said pointedly, crossing her arms over her chest in an unmistakable gesture of feminine pique.

Matt's brows pulled together in confusion, and he hissed at the explosion that involuntary action set off on the left side of his head, the side that had connected with the butt end of a sawed-off shotgun. "Melanie?"

"You called out to her in your sleep, and now you can't remember even who she is?" Sarah clucked her tongue in disapproval. "Ingrid warned me all about you, Matt Thorne, you and your charming ways."

She said "charming" as if it were on par with "homicidal." Matt frowned at the thought that his lovely nurse might be as virtuous as her appearance suggested. That kind of attitude could take a lot of the fun out of his recuperation. With his good eye fixed on Sarah, he gingerly eased himself into a sitting position, leaning back against the headboard. This had to be Ingrid's idea of a practical joke—saddling him with an Amish nurse.

Sarah Troyer. His brain grudgingly gave forth another tidbit of memory. Ingrid had hired an Amish girl to cook and clean at her newly opened inn in southeastern Minnesota. And she had apparently forearmed the girl with tales of his reputation. As if he would actually ravish the innocent maid! As if he was in any condition to. He groaned a little as pain throbbed through him like a pulse.

"Speaking of Ingrid, maybe you should go get her," he said, thinking he had a bone or two to pick with his sister.

First of all, she had been entirely too high-handed in suggesting the hospital release him into her custody, as if he were a criminal with a history of jumping bail. And then she had carted him down to this rustic little backwater town, when he had a perfectly good condo in Minneapolis and any number of delightful female friends to see to his recovery. There was Nurse Newman and Carrie from radiology and that cute little lab tech—what was her name? Oh, yes, Melanie, *that* Melanie. His sigh of remembered contentment almost drowned out Sarah's tiny reply.

"She isn't here."

"I'm sorry, what did you say?"

Sarah screwed up her courage. It was one thing to have the adventure of caring for an unconscious person and fantasizing a bit in the private theater of her imagination. Confronting the living, breathing, speaking, *half-naked* man was another thing altogether.

The quilt had fallen precariously low as he'd propped himself up, leaving his upper body bare and hinting at the fact that if he wore any drawers at all, they were mighty brief indeed. Sarah jerked her gaze up from the edge of the blanket in an effort to avoid further speculation and almost groaned aloud at the sight of a firmly muscled chest dusted with black curls. Curls that whirled into a line and disappeared beneath the pristine white bandage that had been strapped around and around his ribs to hold the cracked bones in place. And below that bandage was . . . Oh, dear.

"Ingrid isn't here," she squeaked, her gaze darting all around the room in a desperate effort to keep from staring at Matt Thorne's naked chest. "She's gone to Stillwater to deal with an emergency at the inn there."

"When will she be back?" he asked, scratching his chest.

Sarah gulped hard. "D-d-days," she stammered, her head swimming at the implications of her folly. What had she been thinking about, agreeing to stay in the same house with this man? Had she really thought he would remain obligingly asleep for the duration so that she would have to cope with only a figment of her imagination? She had never thought the conscious man would be so . . . compelling, so . . . undressed.

"Days," Matt repeated. "What about John?" She gave him a blank look. "John?"

"John Wood. Ingrid's husband. You know. Tall guy, smokes a pipe."

"Yes, of course I know John," she said in a rush, the apples of her cheeks turning a delicious ripe red. "He is gone to California to do research for one of his travel books."

A smile tugged at Matt's mouth as he realized his little nursemaid was nervous. His radar told him there was a strong signal of attraction here—both ways. It was obvious the prim Miss Troyer didn't know how to deal with it. Her big indigo-blue eyes darted from side to side, up and down, lighting everywhere but on him. Her shyness delighted him and excited him in a way that seemed subtly different from anything he'd known before.

"Having trouble with your contact lenses?" he asked, amusement thrumming through his voice.

"What?" Sarah made the huge mistake of looking at him. He captured her gaze with the magnetic force of his dark eyes and held it.

"You seem to be having some trouble with your eyes."

"My sight is fine," she murmured. As a girl she had always longed for a pair of spectacles because they were the only kind of adornment an Amish girl was allowed. Now she wished for them for a different reason. She could have pulled them off and cleaned them and fiddled with the earpieces, busying her hands and giving herself an excuse to not look at Matt Thorne.

He regarded her with his warm dark eyes, eyes sparkling with mischief and who knew what else. The devil himself probably had eyes just like that; eyes brimming with temptation. Locks of black hair fell across his forehead in a way described as "rakish" in books. Now that he was awake and upright, his injuries weren't nearly so distracting as they had been when he'd been asleep. It had to have something to do with the inner life force of the man, the electricity that glowed in his eyes and hummed in the air around him. Sarah felt it pour over her, exciting her as it went. She took another step back, her cowardice rising inside her like a shield.

"What are we supposed to do while Ingrid is away?" Matt asked. "As if I couldn't come up with a couple of wonderful ideas on the subject."

"I'm to look after the inn," Sarah said. "And you."

"Oh, I like that plan," Matt said, laughter in his eyes and voice. "Just think of the fun we can have together."

Sarah shook a finger at him as if it were a magic wand that could force him to do her bidding. "You are to stay in bed."

"My favorite place to be—provided I'm not alone."

"Well, you're sure going to be alone here," she said tartly, finding a little bit of the sass that had always brought her a glower of disapproval from her father. With this man it only seemed to generate more of his teasing humor.

He chuckled weakly, wincing a bit and laying a hand gingerly against the white bandage that swathed his ribs. "Oh, come on, Sarah. Have pity on a poor cripple. You're not really going to make me stay in bed all alone, are you?"

"You bet." She nodded resolutely.

"Them I'm afraid I'm going to have to make a speedy recovery. I can't stand the idea of having a beautiful nurse and not being able to chase her around the bed."

Beautiful. Sarah did her best to ignore his compliment. To accept a compliment was to accept credit for God's doing. It was *Hochmut*—pride—a sin. She didn't need to be charged with any more of them than she already had. So she brushed aside the warm glow that threatened to blossom inside her and decided to match him teasing for teasing. "The shape you're in, I'll have no trouble getting away."

Matt closed his eyes briefly against his assorted pains. "I'm afraid you're right about that. Tell me, do I look as bad as I feel?"

She gave a little sniff, stepping closer to the bed as her initial skittishness subsided. "I don't suppose you feel as bad as you look, else you'd be dead."

Matt gave her a look. "Gee, don't spare my feelings here, Sarah. Lay it on the line."

"I'm sorry," she said, having the grace to blush. "I'm much too forthright. It's always getting me into trouble."

"Really?" Matt chuckled. "I can't imagine you in trouble."

"Ach, me, I'm in trouble all the time," she admitted, rolling her eyes. A secretive little Mona Lisa smile teased her lips as she stepped closer to the bed.

A sweet, warm feeling flooded through Matt. It wasn't exactly lust. It was . . . liking. Sarah Troyer was beguiling him with her innocence, and he would have bet she didn't have the vaguest idea she was doing it. "What kinds of things get you in trouble?"

Her smile faded and she glanced away. *Wishing for things I shouldn't want. Wanting things I can't have.* But her thoughts remained unspoken. The flush that stained her cheeks with color now was from guilt. She was what she was, and she should be grateful for the things she had, she reminded herself, tamping down the longing that sprang eternal in her soul. Like weeds in a garden, her father would say, they must be torn out by the roots. Somehow, she had never had the heart to dig that deep and tear out all her dreams.

She realized with a start that Matt was watching her, waiting for an answer. "Neglecting my work gets me into trouble," she said quietly, eyes downcast to keep him from seeing any other answers that might be revealed by those too-honest mirrors of her true feelings. "I had best go down and see to making you some supper."

"In a minute," Matt murmured, catching her

by the wrist as she turned to go. Her skin was soft and cool beneath his fingertips, like the finest silk. He'd always had an especially acute sense of touch, and now he picked up the delicate beating of Sarah's pulse as if it were pounding like a jackhammer. He wondered if she would even know what a jackhammer was, and he marveled again at how untouched she seemed to him. He felt like the most jaded cynic in comparison.

She would know nothing about the kind of violence that had disrupted his life. Street gangs and drug wars and inner-city desperation were the trappings of another world, a world far removed from farm life and people who disdained automobiles as being too worldly.

For a moment all the weariness and hopelessness caught up with him, and he wondered what it would be like to just chuck it all, plant a garden and buy a horse. He wondered what Sarah Troyer would think if he told her that. He knew what his friends in Minneapolis would think. They would think he'd gone nuts. Sophisticated, cosmopolitan Dr. Matt Thorne a gentleman farmer? Absurd didn't begin to cover it. His concussion had to be worse than he'd realized, he thought, dismissing the notion.

He wanted to ask Sarah about the shadows that had crossed her face an instant before she

had answered his question. He found he
wanted to know all about her. He wrote it off
as a combination of boredom and natural curiosity, and conveniently ignored the fact that he
was not usually so curious about the deep,
dark secrets of the women in his life.

It wasn't that he was so self-absorbed, he
didn't care. It was more a matter of practical-
ity. His career took precedence over all else in
his life, and it left little time or energy for deep
relationships. He wore his title of hospital Romeo with ease and good humor, and thought
of all-consuming romantic love in only the
most abstract of ways. So when Sarah Troyer
turned back toward him, her eyes as blue as
twin lakes under the sun and as round as quarters, he put the jolt in his chest down to a re-
awakening libido and counted himself lucky to
be among the living.

"I think I might need a little help getting
up," he said, his voice a notch huskier than
usual.

"I think you might need to get your hearing
checked," Sarah said breathlessly. She extricat-
ed her arm from his hold and stepped out of
his reach, absently rubbing her wrist as if she
could erase the tingling his touch had roused.
"You are not to get out of bed."

"You take things too literally," he complained. "I'm not to get out of bed *much*."

"At all."

He gave her the superior look that normally brought bossy nurses to heel and said dryly, "Look, trust me on this. I'm a doctor."

"Yes." Sarah nodded, unmoved. "I can see how well you have healed yourself so far."

"Fine," Matt said, scowling, his doctor's ego not taking well to pointed truths. "Don't help me. I'll manage."

It occurred to him that he would have ordered a patient in his condition to remain in bed, but then he wasn't a garden-variety patient. He was a physician. He knew his own limits—most of the time. He certainly knew one of his limits, and it had been reached. He was getting out of this bed, duty-bound maid or no duty-bound maid.

Taking great care to move slowly, he eased his legs over the edge of the bed and waited for his head to stop swimming. Out of deference to Sarah's undoubtedly delicate sensibilities, he pulled the black-and-purple quilt around himself toga-style, then he took as deep a breath as his taped ribs would allow and rose.

The earth tilted drunkenly beneath his feet and he staggered forward in an effort to keep himself from falling. The quilt dropped away as he reached out to grab onto something— anything—to steady himself. The "something" his hands settled on gasped and squirmed. His eyes locked on Sarah's for an instant, an instant full of shock, surprise, and the unmistakable sparks of attraction, then they both went down in a tangle of arms and legs, quilt, and ankle-length cotton skirt.

Sarah gave a squeal as she landed on her back. Matt groaned as he came down on top of her, pain digging into his ribs and pounding through his head. A red-hot arrow of it shot down his left leg and a blissful blackness began to descend over him, beckoning him toward the peace of unconsciousness, but he fought it off. He sucked a breath in through his teeth, held it, expelled it slowly, all the while willing himself to remain in the land of the living.

After a moment that seemed like an eternity, the pain receded. He slowly became aware of the feminine form cushioning his body. There really was a woman under all those clothes, he thought, mentally taking inventory of full breasts and shapely legs. His hands had settled at the curve of her waist, and he let his fingers trace the angles of it. She was trim but womanly. *Very* womanly, he thought, groaning again, but this time in appreciation as she shifted beneath him, and the points of her nipples grazed his chest through the cotton of her gown.

"Are you all right?" Sarah asked, trying to sound concerned as a whole array of other feelings assaulted her—panic, desire, guilt. Matt Thorne was pressed against the whole

length of her, and while there might have been
some question about his health, there was certainly no question about his gender. She
squirmed frantically beneath him, only managing to come into even more intimate contact
with him. She had automatically grabbed him
as they had fallen, and now she found her
hands gripping the powerful muscles of his
upper arms. His skin was smooth and hot to
the touch, and her fingers itched to explore
more of it. How she managed to push the
thought from her head and speak was beyond
her. "Are you injured?"

"Me?" Matt said dreamily, his thick lashes
drifting down as his smile curved his mouth
upward. "I'm in heaven. How about you?"

"I'm being pinned to the floor by two hundred pounds of dead weight," Sarah said irrita-
bly, using anger to burn away the traitorous
threads of longing. She had no business thinking such . . . such . . . *carnal* thoughts about
this man. She hardly knew him and, even if
she had known him from birth, he was out of
her reach. She had to be content to confine
her secret yearnings to her imagination where
they did no one harm.

"Gee, Sarah, you sure know how to bolster a
man's ego," Matt complained. He raised himself up on one elbow and looked down at her,
one black brow arched sardonically.

It seemed to Sarah that no part of him

needed bolstering, but she didn't have the
chance to tell him that. With a clatter of toe-
nails against the hardwood floor, Blossom arrived on the scene. Ingrid Wood's basset hound
hurled herself into the room, skidding to a halt
beside the heads of the fallen, and set up a terrible howling. Sarah winced. Matt swore liber-
ally and clamped his hands over his ears.
Blossom gulped a breath and flung her head
back again with such force that her front paws
came off the floor. The sound was pitiful,
mournful, but, most especially, it was loud.

"She thinks you're attacking me!" Sarah
yelled at Matt, smacking him on the shoulder.

Blossom snatched another breath and hit a
note that should have shattered every glass in
the house.

Matt rolled carefully off Sarah and struggled
to stand, grabbing hold of the oak nightstand
to steady himself. He sat on the chair beside
the bed, staring in disbelief at the dog as Sarah
pushed herself to her feet as well. Blossom let
out one more good howl, then settled herself
on Sarah's feet, apparently content that the
danger had passed. Looking at the dog, with
her woeful brown eyes and furrowed brow,
Matt found it impossible to believe so much
sound had come from such a little animal. She
looked up at him with her speckled nose and
pendulous lips and sighed with satisfaction of

a job well-done. Sarah bent over and stroked the dog's head.

"Good girl, Blossom."

Blossom beamed, breaking into unrestrained panting, her doggy lips pulling back into an obvious smile.

"Leave it to my sister," Matt said, sticking a finger in his ear and wiggling it back and forth in an effort to restore normal hearing. "She couldn't have a Doberman or a German shepherd or any other self-respecting guard dog that would merely take a chunk out of an intruder. She has to get one that renders its victims permanently hearing impaired. I hope darling Blossom catches her and John in the throes of passion some night."

Sarah chuckled at the thought, but the laughter caught in her throat as her eyes settled on Matt. He was indeed all but naked, wearing nothing except bandages and a pair of teeny-tiny burgundy briefs that left little to her overactive imagination. The air in her lungs turned hot, and her jaw dropped.

"What's the matter?" Matt asked, his voice soft with amusement and something like compassion. "Haven't you seen a man in his underwear before?"

"Only my husband," Sarah murmured. And Samuel Troyer had never looked quite like this. He had certainly never made her feel what she was feeling now—all shivery and weak.

The word hit Matt on the head like a hammer. Husband. He shuddered with dread and disappointment. "You're married?"

"I'm a widow."

"I'm sorry," he said automatically, but with genuine feeling. She seemed too young to even have been married. To be a widow at her age was truly a tragedy. He watched her busily straightening her skirt and apron, dusting off imaginary lint. From the way she avoided his searching gaze, he thought she must still be hurting from her loss. He had no way of knowing what she felt was guilt. "He must have been very young."

"He would have been twenty-five this year . . . like me." Even though it had been a year since he'd gone, she still wished she had been a better wife to him.

"What happened?"

"A farming accident."

"That's a shame. Do you have children?"

She couldn't quite keep from flinching at the question. He meant no harm, she knew. He was trying only to express his concern and his sympathy. He couldn't know the depth of the wound that particular question struck.

"No," she said shortly.

Dislodging the basset hound from her feet, she went to the bed and began straightening the covers with brisk efficiency. She turned the sheet down and fluffed the pillows. She dismissed the topic of her husband and her widowhood so thoroughly, Matt thought he might have imagined the whole interlude, but he knew he wasn't that groggy. And now he knew there was a lot more to Sarah Troyer than blue eyes and innocence.

"Let this be a lesson to you, Matt Thorne," she said. "You had ought to stay in bed. You're not strong enough to be up and around."

"That's probably true," he admitted, taking the black terry robe she thrust in his direction without looking at him. He eased his arms into the sleeves, pulled it around him, and tied the belt. "But I'm afraid some things can't wait— like a trip to the bathroom."

"I'll find you a chamber pot."

"No thanks. No offense, Amish, but I'll walk on my lips before I stoop to using a chamber pot—no pun intended."

Sarah lifted her chin to a sanctimonious angle and intoned her father's favorite words. "Pride goeth before a fall."

"Yeah, well," Matt said, unchastened. "I goeth to the bathroom. Are you going to help me get there, Nurse Troyer, or do I get Blossom the Wonder Dog to drag me?"

Blossom gave an outraged booming bark and darted away, hind feet chasing her front like a child's pull-toy as she disappeared into the dark hallway.

Sarah heaved a much-put-upon sigh and

planted her hands on her hips. "All right. I'll help you. But you'll come back to bed and stay there after?"

"Scout's honor."

"I don't know anything about no Scouts. It's your honor that worries me."

"And well it should," Matt said, doing the best Groucho Marx imitation he could considering he could only waggle one eyebrow.

Sarah just blinked at him, looking mildly bemused.

Matt was crestfallen. His Groucho always won him smiles and giggles. "You don't know the Marx Brothers?"

"I don't think so," Sarah said, handing him his cane. "Do they farm around here or are they from the Twin Cities?"

"Never mind," Matt shook his head and chuckled, utterly charmed by her naïveté and the effect it had on his own slightly tarnished soul.

She was a gem, this Amish girl, a natural pearl. In spite of the dents she put in his ego, she was exactly the bright spot he needed in his life right now, when everything in his day-to-day world seemed bleak and hopeless, when he'd almost given up hope of ever finding any goodness in the world again.

Maybe he'd have to thank Ingrid after all.

2

"Ingrid was right. You are a terrible patient."

Matt froze as he lifted the razor to his cheek. His eyes met Sarah's in the mirror above the sink. She stood in the bathroom doorway, arms crossed over her chest, shoulder braced against the jamb, Blossom sitting on her feet. She wore a dark blue dress identical to what she had on yesterday, a black apron, and a stern look that would have done any head nurse proud.

"Shaving doesn't seem like too strenuous an activity," he said.

Straightening, Sarah lifted one brow and planted her fists on her hips. "No? Well, dangerous is maybe a better word at that. The way your hand is shaking, you'll likely cut your own throat."

She was right. His hand was trembling with the effort of lifting the razor toward his cheek. It amazed him how weak he felt. The trip to the bathroom and back the night before had done him in. The instant he had crawled back in bed and let his head touch the pillow he'd been unconscious, and he'd remained that way until the buttery light of morning had peeked in around the edges of his window shade.

He had expected to feel stronger with the dawn of a new day, and he had managed the walk to the bathroom himself with the aid of his cane. But now he stood leaning heavily against the oak vanity, his heart beating a little too fast, his breathing a little too labored, his hand shaking in a way that made his razor look as safe as a chain saw.

He managed a smile as he met Sarah's eyes in the mirror again. "If I did myself in with this thing, would you be sad?"

"You bet," she said, teasing lights brightening her eyes, her Mona Lisa smile curling up one corner of her mouth. "Think of the mess I'd have to clean up."

"You're the soul of sympathy."

"You don't deserve sympathy if you're not going to follow your doctor's orders."

He shook his razor at her, narrowing his eyes. "You could go far in the nursing profession. Or as a marine. The requirements are similar."

Sarah sniffed at him, working at looking annoyed. He was teasing her, of course, but she had, in fact, once fantasized about becoming a nurse . . . or a teacher . . . or an astronaut. When she was twelve, she had fantasized about becoming a spy because she had been pretty sure spies got to go all over the world. But at twenty-five she knew it was not likely she would become any of those things no matter how one foolish corner of her heart still wished for it. Because of her ties to her family, she would always be just an Amish girl. Overseeing the recuperation of the dashing Dr. Thorne was probably as exciting as her life was ever going to get.

Matt watched her carefully in the mirror. She did an admirable job of maintaining her stern expression, but she couldn't stop her eyes from looking wide and vulnerable and a little bit sad. He had only been teasing her, as he had teased every female he'd ever known, but he'd struck some hidden chord inside her, and she didn't want him to know it. *Too bad, Sarah,* he thought. *I'm beginning to want to know everything about you.*

"I guess I'm not used to being on the other side of the stethoscope," he admitted, setting his razor down and bracing himself against the sink with both hands as a little more of his strength seeped away. He wasn't used to having anything wrong with him. He had always been athletic and fit, and took his good health for granted. Now his body seemed like a hostile stranger to him, refusing to cooperate with his will. It was frustrating. It was also giving him a new sympathy for his own patients. "As

a rule, doctors don't make very good patients,"
he said.

Sarah's brows knitted in confusion at the
paradox of a doctor who wouldn't take care of
his own health. "What good is all that learning
if a person won't make use of it on themself?"

He mustered a wry smile. "Good question.
Unfortunately, we doctors tend to think we're
immune to pain and suffering. We're too
wrapped up in taking care of everyone else. It
makes us think we're superhuman."

"You don't look so super now," she said
dryly.

"Thank you," Matt said, scowling. "All this
encouraging flirtation is doing wonders for my
morale."

Sarah stepped into the bathroom and picked
up the razor and a thick terry towel. "Back to
bed with you, Matt Thorne. I will do the shaving."

She smiled blandly at Matt's skeptical look
and handed him his cane. He was ridiculously
appealing with his dark eyes scowling at her,
and shaving cream lathered over the lower
half of his face like a frothy white beard. He
wore a rumpled gray T-shirt that clung to his
wide shoulders, and navy blue shorts that
bared strong-looking hairy legs. High up on
his left thigh was a bandage that matched the
one around his ribs. Her gaze lingered there a

moment before she jerked it back up to his face.

"Like what you see, Blue Eyes?" he asked in a voice so soft and seductive, it was like a caress on Sarah's senses.

She swallowed hard and gave him what she hoped was a steely glare. "I'll like it better when I see it in bed."

Matt put a hand to his chest and feigned shock. "Miss Troyer! Such frankness leaves me lightheaded!"

Sarah blushed as she realized just how he had deliberately taken her remark. He was no doubt a master at word games and all the subtleties of flirtation. Ingrid had remarked more than once that her brother was a notorious ladies' man. Sarah could hold her own when teasing, but she knew she was in over her head with Matt Thorne in more ways than one.

"If you took that as an invitation, then you must be delirious," she said dryly.

"Hopeful," Matt corrected her, delighted in the way she rose to the challenge of sparring with him. He wouldn't have expected so much spunk from an Amish girl. His mental image of the Amish was one of somber austerity. It had never occurred to him that they might have a sense of humor.

"Hope*less*," Sarah said with that beguiling little mysterious smile curling her lips. She

pointed to the door that led directly into his
room and gave him a meaningful look.

"Give a poor invalid the comfort of believing
beautiful women still want him," Matt said
over his shoulder as he thumped away from
the sink, leaning heavily on his cane. "A man
needs a reason to live, you know."

As if there was any question women would
find him attractive, Sarah thought. Even
beat-up Matt Thorne was the most desirable
man she'd ever encountered. She gave herself
the luxury of studying him as he made his way
slowly across the bedroom. The perfect width
of his shoulders was emphasized by his
T-shirt. His back tapered to trim hips, to— She
jerked her gaze upward again and fastened it
on the back of his head. His black hair was
tousled, reminding her he had just gotten out
of bed.

She, on the other hand, had been up for
hours. In truth, she could have saved herself
the trouble of going to bed at all, she'd gotten
so little sleep. No matter what mundane or
spiritual matter she had tried to concentrate
on, her thoughts had turned again and again
to the man sleeping just down the hall from
her—his smile, his teasing, the feel of him
against her. Thoughts like that would only lead
to trouble, she knew, but she had never had
much success at squelching her imagination.
She had always resented the need to try. It

didn't seem a sin to her to appreciate God's handiwork. The Almighty had done a fine job with Matt Thorne. What was the point if He hadn't meant for others to notice?

The word temptation crossed her mind, but she dismissed it. If the Lord had not meant for men and women to notice each other, then He wouldn't have made them so different in such interesting ways, she reasoned.

Of course, his maleness wasn't the only thing that made Matt a temptation. Sarah's heart squeezed a little at the thought of what it would do to her family if she gave in to her inner yearnings and became involved with an Englishman like Matt Thorne. They would be so hurt. All her life she had been something of a disappointment to her father because of her insatiable yearnings for things she was not supposed to have. To want Matt Thorne, to succumb to that want would be her ultimate sin in Isaac Maust's eyes. She would be cut off from her family, from her people. Her standing with her father was tenuous at the best of times, so she could easily imagine life without him, but her mother was a different story. And her sister, Ruth, and brothers Daniel and Lucas and Peter and Jacob. Most especially she would miss Jacob; he was more like a son to her than a brother.

It was a moot point, at any rate, she told herself as she watched Matt settle himself carefully on the bed with his back against the high-carved oak headboard, and his legs stretched out on top of the rumpled covers. What would a worldly man like Matt Thorne want with a little Amish country mouse like her?

"Are you sure you know how to do this?" he asked, eyeing her nervously as she set a bowl of water on the nightstand.

"I used to shave my grandfather after his eyesight failed," she said by way of an answer as she leaned over him and draped a towel across his chest.

Matt's thoughts wandered for an instant while he appreciated the proximity of Sarah's breasts. Now that he knew the shape of them by touch, the fact that her garb hid them didn't hinder his imagination any. He pictured them as fitting perfectly in his hands, plump and firm like ripe peaches with dusky nipples that would pout for his attention.

"I thought Amish men wore beards," he said hoarsely as she moved to pick up the razor.

"In our order they do wear beards once they marry." She settled on the edge of the bed, facing him, and her breath caught as her hip pressed against his thigh. "But they wear no . . ."

The word escaped her as her gaze met Matt's. The awareness in those dark eyes sent her heart racing. To her credit, she tried to

gather her wits and hold on to the thread of
the conversation. "They don't wear . . . um . . ."
When she lifted a finger and traced the line of
his upper lip, electricity sizzled through her,
shooting like lightning from her fingertip to
all the most feminine parts of her body. "Um,
mustache," she mumbled breathlessly, too
rattled to realize she had used the Amish pro-
nunciation.

Matt watched the parade of emotions passing over Sarah's face. She was attracted to him
and that attraction frightened her. The chival-
rous part of him, the gentleman, wanted to reassure her. But he couldn't quite separate the
need to reassure from the need to hold her.
She was pretty and sweet and a breath of fresh
air. And his own emotions seemed to be rocking. It was true, he genuinely liked all kinds of
women, but the fact of the matter was he only
played with the ones who knew the rules. He
doubted Sarah Troyer would even realize it
was a game. Still, he didn't see the harm in
flirting with her a little.

Her fingertip was still lingering in the foam
along the bow of his upper lip, teasing him,
tempting him. He caught her delicate wrist
and drew her hand downward so that the finger in question skipped over his upper lip
and landed firmly on the lower one. He drew
his tongue across it, watching with pure male
satisfaction as Sarah's eyes widened and

darkened, and her cheeks flushed with the unmistakable color of desire. The look of panic that followed that automatic sexual response hit Matt like a whip and he released her hand.

A teasing light sparkled in his eyes as he said, "When I was a kid, I always thought this stuff would taste like whipped cream. It tastes like Styrofoam."

Sarah made no comment, but set about the business of shaving him, alternately worrying she might cut him because her hand was less than steady and entertaining thoughts of deliberately doing him in for unleashing such raw desires in her.

Of course, it wasn't his fault she was not content with her life, she reflected as she carefully avoided the stitches on his chin. She couldn't see that it was anyone's fault really; it just was. She hadn't asked to have this yearning to learn or to experience or to want excitement. It was something that had always been in her, something she had had to struggle to subdue her whole life. Matt Thorne set it off like a match struck to dry tinder, but that wasn't his fault.

Her father would have something different to say on the matter, she was sure. His opinions of the English and their evil, tempting ways were well-known. But then, she had no intention of telling him about Matt Thorne or her desires. The less he knew about her job at Thornewood Inn, the better. He was already unhappy about it. Thankfully, the money she was contributing to the farm had diluted his dislike so far.

"Sarah?"

The sound of her name jolted her from her thoughts. She stared at Matt, knowing he had asked her a question that she hadn't heard. "I'm sorry. What?"

"I asked how you came to work here. I admit I don't know much about the Amish, but I wouldn't have thought Amish girls were allowed to work outside their own community."

"Oh, sure," she said, making light of what was a very touchy issue among her people. "We can take jobs so long as they don't go against the teachings of the church."

"But your people don't believe in using electricity or indoor plumbing, do they? You use those things here. Doesn't that go against the church?"

"We don't have those conveniences because we believe they act as corrupting influences on the family, but we don't claim they're evil nor do we begrudge others having them," she explained. Personally, she had never understood how a toilet could corrupt anybody, but she kept her opinion to herself. "Hold still now or you'll be short a nose."

It was only after she had finished shaving

him that Sarah brought up the one question she had been wanting most to ask Matt. She sat back with the damp towel wound around her hands. She knew she should move to the chair beside the bed, but she had grown comfortable sitting next to him, and in truth she enjoyed the small tingle of pleasure that came from her hip brushing against his leg.

"Ingrid told me you'd been injured in some kind of attack, but I didn't understand."

That makes two of us, Matt thought. He considered himself sophisticated, worldly, experienced. Still he had a difficult time dealing with the senseless violence of gang warfare. He couldn't imagine how he was going to explain it to Sarah. He wasn't sure he wanted to. But she sat beside him, waiting patiently, looking so eager to learn something about the Big World.

"I'm in charge of the emergency room at a hospital in the Cities," he began. "It's a county hospital in what has become a very bad part of town. We see a lot of victims of crimes, a lot of criminals." He broke off, frustrated. "Do you know what street gangs are?"

She nodded solemnly. "I read about them in Ingrid's *Newsweek* magazine."

The idea of Sarah reading *Newsweek* threw him for a moment, but he shook it off and went back to his explanation. "Well, gangs have been growing in the Minneapolis area over the last five or six years. Gangs from Chicago and Los Angeles are moving in, calling it 'Moneyapolis' because of the potential for profit they see there. Consequently, we're starting to see a lot of gang-related crime and violence.

"This time it happened right in my emergency room—with me in the middle of it. The Disciples and the Vice Lords got into a little disagreement over a drug deal." He pointed to the bruise above his left eye. "I got hit here with the butt of a shotgun. This is where I connected with the edge of a cabinet," he said, indicating the stitches on his chin. "I've got three cracked ribs, and the bandage on my leg is hiding a nice big bullet hole."

His account was a much-tidied version of the explosion of violence and hatred that had rocked the ER that night. He deleted the blood and gore and the fact that a sixteen-year-old Vice Lord had ended the evening as a corpse. He didn't tell Sarah that an innocent child had been wounded by flying glass from a broken cabinet door or that he himself had sustained a concussion and a bruised kidney in addition to his other injuries. He could see that the G-rated version had upset her enough.

Sarah felt herself go pale as Matt calmly tallied his injuries. He was so matter-of-fact about it. The idea of that kind of violence shook her to her very core. That one human being could do such terrible things to another was beyond her understanding. She had lived such a sheltered life, a life narrowly structured around faith and family. And she had wanted for so long to escape that rigid structure and explore the world beyond. It frightened her something fierce to know such awful things happened in that world she was so eager to discover. She tended to think of it in wonderful terms, that it was full of amazing things to learn and experience, when it undoubtedly held equal amounts of suffering and evil. Whenever that realization struck her, she felt naive and foolish, and now she felt fear for Matt as well.

"You could have been killed," she murmured, shivering at the thought.

Matt looked at her with sympathy for her now-sullied naiveté. "Yeah," he said softly, reaching out to cover her small hand with his.

Funny, he thought, that he was the one who had been attacked, but it was Sarah who needed comforting. And it was odd how good it felt to give that little bit of comfort. He had been trying so long to make a difference in the world by patching up the wounded and sending them back out into the war. Yet just this one small gesture made him feel better. Maybe he had given up thinking the world could be saved by his meager efforts. Maybe he had seen too much of people who had lost all respect for humanity. He had certainly seen far too much of needless suffering and senseless death. And here was this one simple, sweet Amish woman, touched by his pain. He wanted to kiss her just for caring.

Hell, he just plain wanted to kiss her.

"You know what I could use, Nurse Troyer?" he said softly, trying to coax a smile out of her.

Sarah shrugged, too shaken to trust her voice.

"Some breakfast. I'm starved."

She nodded and managed a tiny smile. "Ya, a good big breakfast. You need your strength for healing."

She moved to rise, but the pressure of Matt's hand on hers kept her seated beside him. Her heart did a little flip as she looked down at the sight of her small hand engulfed in his. His was wide and capable looking with blunt-tipped fingers and neatly manicured nails. It felt warm and gentle, and she suddenly couldn't remember the last time she'd been touched that way.

Seemingly with a will of its own, her hand turned over and rubbed palm against palm with Matt's. The friction generated a heat that sizzled through her, burning her breath away in her lungs and igniting fires in all her most secret womanly places. It should have felt forbidden, but it didn't. It felt good. She felt alive.

She could sense Matt's dark eyes searching her expression, and she made a little face and pulled her hand back to the relative safety of her own lap.

"You have no calluses," she said quietly. It came out sounding like an accusation, as if it were a wicked, sexy secret he had deliberately kept from her.

"I get paid a lot of money to keep these hands as soft as a baby's."

"It seems strange to me," she admitted. "Most of the men I know are farmers. Even their wives have calluses."

"I can't afford them. As a doctor my sense of touch has to be sensitive, acute. I have to be able to read people with my hands," Matt said. "Here. I'll show you."

Sarah sat as still and wary as a doe, watching him as he lifted his hands to cup her face. He closed his eyes, thick dark lashes sweeping down like lace fans. His fingertips stroked along the surface of her skin like a whisper, following the ripe curve of her cheek, the line of her jaw. The pads of his thumbs brushed the outer corners of her mouth, and her lips parted in unconscious invitation.

"Beautiful," he whispered. "Delicate. Sweet."

His fingertips slid into the soft tendrils of hair that curled down along the nape of her neck, and he drew her forward gently, inexorably, so that she felt more like she was falling than being pulled toward him. Her own eyes drifted shut, lulled by the sensuous spell he had cast over her. And his lips brushed over hers with as light a touch as his fingers', sampling, tasting.

"Sweet," he murmured again, the word itself a kiss.

For Sarah, time stood absolutely still, and she was aware of everything about the moment: Matt, the warm, minty taste of him, the feel of his hands cradling her head, the softness of his mouth, the scent of fall drifting in through the window on a warm Indian summer breeze, the rustling of the dry leaves on the big maple tree that stood beside the house, the crack of a branch, and the surprised cry—

Sarah bolted from the bed. "What on earth?"

Blossom hurled herself across the room, howling like a hunting hound in full cry. She reached the open window just before Sarah, flinging her front half onto the sill, and her speckled nose up against the screen.

"Bow-ooooo! Bow-ooooo!"

With her hands clamped to her ears, Sarah peered out, scanning the tree limbs for signs of life. At the base, a pile of brilliant orange leaves began to move. And suddenly a small blond head poked through, and she was staring down into the wide blue eyes of her baby brother.

3

"Jacob!"

"Hello, Sarah!" the boy called, giving her a merry grin that revealed two dark gaps where teeth were missing. One small hand emerged from the pile of leaves to wave up at her. "I come to visit with you."

Sarah muttered a prayer in German under her breath and pressed a hand to her pounding heart. "Are you hurt?"

"Not so much as I might have been," he conceded. "In my coat I tore a hole," he said, his English translation of German thoughts spoken slightly out of order.

He pulled back a flap of dark cloth along his left elbow to illustrate the point for his sister. The blue cotton shirt beneath his jacket had fared no better. Jacob's brows knitted together in belated concern as he took notice of the bloody scrape on his arm.

"Stay right where you are, young man!" Sarah ordered, pulling back from the window.

Matt was already out of bed, thumping around the room with his cane, searching for something.

Sarah glared at him. "And just what do you think you're doing?"

"Someone's hurt. I'm a doctor. I'm going to help," he said in a voice that brooked no disagreement. He yanked open the closet door and shoved aside half a dozen shirts, hangers singing along the iron rod. "Where's my medical bag? Don't tell me Ingrid didn't pack my medical bag."

"Fine," Sarah muttered through her teeth. "I won't tell you."

It seemed futile to try to stop Matt now that he had already gotten out of bed. The horse was out of the barn, and she had more important things to do than chase him. She had to get to her brother. She had no idea how far Jacob had fallen. He might have broken something or injured himself inside. A hundred terrible fears sprang up in Sarah's throat. She rushed out the door of the bedroom and down the stairs with Blossom hot on her heels, the long-bodied hound negotiating the steps like a Slinky.

A shaggy chestnut pony grazed unattended in the front yard. Sarah ran past him, a handful of skirt and apron knotted in her fist to keep the garments from tangling around her legs. Jacob sat exactly where he had fallen. The boy was chest-deep in fallen leaves, but he didn't look so pleased about his predicament as he had initially. He was cradling his arm against him and trying valiantly not to cry. Big, bright tears swam in his eyes, and his mouth trembled in spite of the fact that he had pulled his lower lip between his teeth and was biting down for all he was worth.

Sarah hurled herself to her knees in the leaves in front of him. "Let me see, *bobbli*," she said gently, her voice trembling as much as her hands as she reached out toward him.

"I'm not a baby," Jacob snapped. He twisted away from her, more out of fear of pain than defiance. "It's just a scrape is all."

"How about letting me be the judge of that?" Matt suggested.

He was winded and pale, half-dizzy from trying to descend the stairs faster than was prudent for a man in his condition. But he managed what he thought would pass for a brave face and gratefully sank to his knees in the cushion of the leaf pile.

Jacob stared at him with owl eyes. "Who are you?"

"My name is Matt. I'm a doctor."

"You're English."

"If that means I'm not Amish, then I guess you're right. Is that okay with you?" Matt struggled to maintain a sober face as he asked. The boy was adorable, maybe seven or eight with yellow hair and a dusting of freckles across his impudent nose. The smile he gave Matt was a smaller version of Sarah's, but his eyes gleamed with sudden excitement rather than dry amusement.

"Ya, sure," Jacob said, looking Matt up and down with wonder. "You ain't wearing no trousers," the boy observed.

"Jacob! Your manners!" Sarah hissed, her sense of propriety all mixed up amongst her fears. Her heart was still going a hundred miles an hour at the idea of her baby falling from a tree. She had been the one to look after Jacob most of his young life. Their mother had taken ill after his birth, and Sarah, who had no baby of her own, had gladly seen to Jacob's care. She had never grown out of thinking of him more as a son than a brother.

Matt took no offense at the boy's lack of manners. He scooted a little nearer Jacob. "Nope. These are my lucky running shorts. Want to know why they're lucky?"

The blond head bobbed.

"Because I used to wear them all the time back in college when I ran in races."

"What is this college? Is it a town?"

The question knocked Matt speechless for an instant, until it occurred to him that the Amish probably didn't go in for higher education. "It's the kind of school a guy has to go to if he wants to become a doctor," he explained.

"And did you win the races?" Jacob asked, typically unconcerned with the idea of school.

Races, however, were of great interest. He stared up at Matt, waiting for his response, unconsciously relaxing his hold on his injured arm.

"Sometimes," Matt said, slowly reaching out. "Let's have a look at this. So you like to climb trees, do you? I used to be the champion tree climber on my block when I was a kid. The second best tree climber was a girl. Can you believe that?"

"No." Jacob pulled back a little as Matt's fingers closed around his wrist, but he slowly relaxed and straightened out the arm. "I don't know any girls can climb trees except for Sarah."

"Is that a fact?" Matt shot Sarah a surprised grin and chuckled at the blush that crept across her cheeks. "I'd like to see that."

"Jonah Yoder is the best tree climber I know," Jacob went on, warming to the topic, forgetting all about Matt examining his arm. "He's ten and he can climb like a squirrel. I can climb pretty good, but sometimes my reach is not far enough. I'm only eight and I'm not so big as Jonah Yoder is."

Sarah leaned in to get a look at the scrape, her expression worried. "Is it broken?"

"Heck no, it's just a scrape," Matt said, rolling his eyes at Jacob. "Girls."

"Girls," Jacob parroted derisively. He gave

his sister a superior look. "Heck no, Sarah. It's not broke."

"It's a doozy of a scrape, though," Matt said. "Really gross."

"What is this gross?" the boy asked.

"Gross is like *really* yucky looking," Matt explained, making a face that indicated it was something a boy could appreciate in a way no one else could. It was a look that breached the culture barrier. Gross was a concept relished by all boys everywhere, even if they didn't use the same word for it.

Jacob eyed his wound with new delight. "Gross," he said, obviously liking the way the new word sat on his tongue. He looked up at Matt and they both grinned.

"Radically gross!"

Jacob giggled. "Rad-ic-cally gross!"

"We'll have to clean it up and put some goop on it," Matt said, sobering.

The boy looked up at him, suddenly not so brave. "Will it hurt so very much?"

"Nothing a champion tree climber like you can't handle. At least you won't need stitches, like I did," Matt said, showing off the line on his chin.

Jacob's eyes widened in a horrified awe. "Did you get that falling out of a tree?"

"No. I had a little accident at work."

Sarah helped her brother up, clucking at him and muttering in German as she dusted the leaves off him and herself. She scooped up his wide-brimmed felt hat and clamped it on his head. Matt struggled to his feet and leaned heavily against his cane for a moment as the world swayed around him.

"Maybe we can get Sarah to whip us up some breakfast while you and I get that arm taken care of."

Sarah glanced up, her stomach clenching at the sight of Matt, pale and wobbly. "Run along into the kitchen, Jacob. Sit at the table and wait for us, and no playing with the toaster." As the boy scampered off, she took a step toward Matt. "Are you all right?"

"Sure," he said, forcing a weak version of his sexy grin. "I'm still a little light-headed from that kiss is all."

She looked at him as if he'd just insulted her, turned on her heel, and hurried off toward the house with a rustle of skirts.

Matt watched her go, bemused. Flight wasn't the usual effect he had on women. He scratched his throbbing head and frowned down at Blossom, who had come to root through the leaves like a hog sniffing for truffles. The kiss he had shared with Sarah had stunned him. It had been the lightest of kisses, almost chaste, but the electricity had darn near knocked his socks off. She had to have felt it too.

Well, he was feeling too weak to think about

the mysteries of the female mind just now, let alone try to subjugate them. And there was an injury to tend to. Dredging up the last of his energy reserves, he started toward the house, almost tripping over the basset hound that had settled herself on his feet.

"Why aren't you in school today?" Sarah asked as she unloaded first aid supplies from her arms onto the pine harvest table in the sunny, spacious kitchen.

Jacob jumped back from the counter where he had been fingering the trigger of the shiny chrome four-slot toaster. "Our teacher has the croup so we don't have no school."

"You haven't any school," Sarah corrected.

"Nope."

"What? No substitute teacher?" Matt asked, motioning Jacob to have a seat on the table.

"There is only one teacher in our Amish school," Sarah explained. "We have none in reserve."

"And I suppose this is a one-room school-house with privies out back," Matt said, half-joking.

Sarah gave him a cool look, her chin lifting. "Of course."

Embarrassed, Matt wished he could disappear into the linoleum. But seeing no graceful way out of his blunder, he simply ignored it, clearing his throat and turning attention to

Jacob once again. He cleaned the boy's scrape, his touch as delicate as he could keep it as he worked out the bits of tree bark and dried leaf.

Sarah hovered at his elbow, looking ready to throw herself between them at the first sign of any real pain from her brother. Every time Jacob winced, Sarah flinched and sucked in a little gasp. For every stray tear that squeezed its way out of Jacob's eyes, Sarah shed two. Matt watched her out of the corner of his eye, torn between amusement, sympathy, and annoyance.

"I'm just cleaning it and applying a dressing," he said. "This isn't an amputation we're talking about here. And I assure you, I know what I'm doing. I'll have you know I graduated fourth in my class from the University of Minnesota med school."

"How many was in it?" Sarah asked, not quite joking.

Matt gave her a look. "Very funny. Why don't you sit down before you pass out? Or better yet, get started on that breakfast you promised me."

She cast an anxious glance at Jacob, who was more interested in playing with the dispenser of adhesive tape. She forced herself to back away, step by agonizing step, gnawing on her lip and blinking back tears.

"Your confidence in me is overwhelming," Matt said sarcastically. "Take some comfort in knowing I can't run away from you. If I screw up, you can pummel me to a bloody pulp with the bludgeon of your choice." He turned to Jacob and made a face. "Girls. You'd think she'd never seen anything gross before."

Jacob sniffled and giggled and swung his feet over the table edge.

While Sarah set to work on the breakfast, Matt and Jacob settled themselves at the table and discussed things of interest to boys. Mostly Jacob told Matt everything he knew about farming, how good the corn crop looked, how they were getting ready to harvest, and how he was going to help. He talked a steady blue streak, and Matt looked grave and nodded at appropriate intervals. Sarah watched them out of the corner of her eye, thinking Matt was awfully sweet for listening and asking questions. He probably didn't give a hoot about how dry the corn was, but he paid attention as if it were of great importance to him.

What a good father he would make, she thought, wishing she could ignore the sweet pang of longing in her breast. She set Matt's breakfast down in front of him, along with a steaming cup of coffee, trying not to think about the comfortable domesticity of the scene.

"Does Mom know you are here?" Sarah asked Jacob as she handed him a glass of milk and set a plate of oatmeal-raisin cookies on the kitchen table.

Jacob eyed the cookies like a starving creature, reaching slowly for the biggest one even though he hadn't asked permission. "Ya," he said. "I had done my chores and Pop said for me to come visit with you."

"Did he?" Sarah murmured more to herself than to Jacob. She couldn't stop the little rush of temper that spurted up inside her. Isaac hadn't sent his youngest son to merely keep her company or to keep him out of the way on the farm. He had been sent as an unwitting observer. Jacob would eagerly relate all he had seen at the English inn. Sarah would never ask him not to. Her job was her own. She did nothing here to be ashamed of.

Her glance darted to Matt, and guilt slapped splashes of color high across her cheeks. They had kissed. She'd sat right on his bed and let him kiss her.

And Jacob had been scrambling up the tree just outside the window.

"Why were you climbing that tree?" she asked.

Her brother's eyes were round and innocent. He shrugged and talked around a mouthful of cookie. "Because it was there."

"The perfect reason," Matt said with a grin.

With the enthusiasm of a lumberjack, he ate the breakfast Sarah had fixed him. It had been

ages since he'd had a big, calorie-laden, homemade breakfast. He usually took no time for
breakfast, grabbing a peanut butter sandwich
or a bagel on his way to the hospital. With his
strength at low tide, however, he had no trouble convincing himself that he needed something more substantial. The eggs and fried
potatoes and toast went down nicely.

He reached for a cookie and shook it at his
new little *compadre*. "You'll have to be a little
more careful next time, pal. Climbing trees is a
lot of fun, but it's a long way down and there
isn't always a pile of leaves handy to land on."

Jacob nodded as he drank, some milk
sloshing out to dribble down his chin. He
wiped it off with his good arm and chomped
another bite out of his cookie.

Sarah settled herself in her chair and set
herself to the task of mending the tear in her
brother's jacket sleeve.

"How far up were you?" she asked, feeling
like a weasel for trying to wheedle information
out of him. She was no better than her father
was for sending him here. Poor Jacob.

"Not far."

"This is not the place for you to be climbing
trees," she scolded, more cross with herself
than with her brother. "The Woods often have
guests here who would not appreciate looking
out their windows to see little Amish boys staring in at them."

So that was what the interrogation was all about, Matt mused, chewing thoughtfully on his cookie. Sarah was afraid her brother might have caught them kissing. Strange. She was a grown woman. She'd been married for heaven's sake. What difference would it make if someone saw them kissing?

He watched her as she worked the needle and thread through the fabric of the coat with vicious stabs and jerks that betrayed her inner agitation. Several strands of silky brown hair had escaped the stranglehold of the bun at the back of her head and drifted down along her cheek into her line of sight. She tucked them back up under her *kapp* without looking up. She looked like a living work of art—"Study of a Nineteenth-century Woman." A nineteenth-century woman with nineteenth-century sensibilities.

That was it. She was shy, reserved. The idea appealed to Matt in a way he wouldn't have expected. He was used to women who knew the score, women who moved at a nineteen-nineties pace, women who often as not took the lead in a physical relationship. Compared to them, Sarah was untouched, untried, innocent. Once again he felt a strong surge of protectiveness swell inside him, and tenderness . . . and desire.

He wasn't going to be able to act on any of those impulses at the moment, however, he realized with no small amount of regret. Ordinarily, he was relentless in his pursuit of something he wanted—especially when that something was a lady. But his exertions that morning had drained him. Fatigue weighed down on him like an anvil, pressing on his throbbing head, causing the muscles in his shoulders to tense. His ribs were aching, and the wound in his thigh was burning. He needed to lie down before he simply fell out of his chair and sprawled unconscious on the kitchen floor.

"Well, folks," he announced, carefully standing up. "I think I'd better get back to bed. All this excitement has worn me out," he said, sending Sarah a warm, meaningful look that caused her to frown and blush.

"You English sure keep strange habits," Jacob said, reaching for his third cookie.

Sarah batted his hand away from the plate, scowling at him. "Have they set you out to live with the pigs at home? You have such manners."

Jacob blushed.

"I don't usually spend the day in bed," Matt explained, unperturbed. "I'm just not feeling so good right now."

"Maybe you need some castor oil," Jacob suggested. "That's what Mom always gives me."

Matt grimaced. "I think I'll pass on that for now."

"When you are better, Matt Thorne, I will show you how I ride my pony," the boy said earnestly. "You can come to the farm. To the calves I will show you. It's my job to feed them and help clean their pens."

"Gross," Matt said with a wink.

Jacob giggled.

Sarah heaved a sigh and stuck herself accidentally with her needle.

The rest of the day did not go according to the Laws of Dr. Thorne, and Matt didn't care for it a bit. He was too used to being the boss, to being in control. Being an invalid did not sit well. Everything seemed to irritate him. The room was too light, too dark, he missed the noises of the city, he missed the energy, he missed being busy, he missed being able to do whatever he wanted to with his body.

He had gone upstairs after breakfast with the mistaken idea that a little nap would restore the strength he had spent that morning. He'd slept for six hours, awakened only long enough to take his medication and complain a little, then he'd gone under again.

This was no way to win a lady.

It was especially no way to win a lady who wouldn't stick around long enough for him to charm her. Sarah had made herself scarce,

leaving only a little bell on the nightstand in
her stead.

Matt plumped up the pillows behind him
and settled back. He could smell supper cooking. The scent of meat and potatoes drifted se-
ductively up the stairs. Sarah was down in the
kitchen cooking for him. What a good wife she
would make. Not that he was looking for a
wife or knew anything about wives specifically.
He'd never been in the market for one himself.
It just seemed to him that Sarah would be
good at all the traditional wife things. Well,
she had been a wife, hadn't she?

He had always been too busy working to
think about marriage. He'd spent far more
time at the hospital in the last six years than
he had at his apartment.

And for what? a cynical voice questioned
deep inside him. The words seemed to echo in
a hollow cavern in his chest. Once he'd been
full of smart answers to that question. Now he
just sat there feeling burned out and anxious
all at once. He loved being a doctor. He loved
having people look to him for help and being
able to help them. It was just that something
vital was missing now and he didn't know
what to do about it. He missed the bustle of
the hospital and yet a part of him didn't want
to go back. For the first time in his life he
didn't really know what he wanted.

Supper, he thought, pushing the fears and

uncertainties from his mind with an ill-tempered shove. He wanted supper and he wanted company. He rang the little bell on the stand, then winced as Blossom rushed into the room and howled at him, apparently taking exception to the high-pitched sound.

"Why couldn't Ingrid have a cat?" he asked crossly, as Sarah appeared in the doorway with a dinner tray.

Sarah frowned at him. Blossom frowned at him. Matt rolled his eyes and pouted.

"I hate being sick," he complained as Sarah placed the tray across his lap. "I hate the idea that someone else is running my ER, seeing my patients—"

"Flirting with your nurses?"

He glanced up at her as she shook out the proper dose of his various medications into her hand. Her mouth quirked at the corners with that knowing little smile, but the expression in her eyes was soft and a little uncertain. What a bundle of contradictions she was—innocence and sass; a woman in most respects, but with such an air of naiveté about her. She fascinated him and that fascination took the edge off his foul mood. Something about just having her in the room made him feel more relaxed.

His gaze drifted from her hands with their trimmed, unpolished nails to her breasts, to the bottom lip she pulled between her teeth as she fought with the safety cap on one of the pill bottles. Desire stirred lazily in his groin. Maybe relaxed wasn't exactly the word.

"I'll have you know, flirting is a very serious business where I come from," he said.

"Hmmm. Well, you've been getting plenty of practice here then, haven't you?"

He swallowed the pills she gave him and washed them down with water. The delectable meal on the tray drew his attention, and he let his gaze wander over it as he spoke. "There's no such thing as too much practice. Perfection is strived for but never achieved."

Sarah gave him a look that told him she wasn't swallowing any of his malarkey. It was a practiced look, one she had perfected as a defense to keep people from thinking they could get the better of her.

"Enjoy your supper," she said, forcing herself to take a step toward the door. "Just ring when you want me to come take the tray away."

Matt felt a pang in his midsection that had nothing to do with his cracked ribs. "You're not leaving already, are you? Why don't you stay awhile and let me work on my bedside manner?"

"You're on the wrong side of the bed," Sarah pointed out.

He gave her his most winning, devilish smile, the one that always made the nurses—

even the starchiest ones—giggle. "That all depends on your point of view, Amish."

Sarah looked down at him, impossibly handsome and rumpled, his dark eyes twinkling. She thought of his reputation and her reckless streak and the stricken looks her family would give her. She thought of the sheltered world in which she lived and the violent, sophisticated one Matt Thorne dealt with every day with a wink and a grin. And she saw very clearly that there was a point where her little adventure would become something she wouldn't be able to handle.

She came to the conclusion that while Matt Thorne was worldly enough to play word games and tease and kiss her without meaning anything by it, she was not worldly at all. And the needs she kept so carefully leashed inside her had been too long denied to resist much temptation. Matt was a ladies' man; Ingrid had told her as much. But she was not a lady. She was just a plain young woman who wanted too many things she couldn't have. Matt would stay here until he was healed and then he would leave, and she would be the one left hurting.

"I have other duties to see to," she said softly. It was almost a fib, but she didn't think almost should count for much. There were pots to wash and dusting to do. Mainly there

was her virtue to safeguard and her heart to
protect.

"There can't be that much," Matt protested.
"How many other guests are staying here right
now?"

"None. But four are coming for the weekend
and there are things that must be done."

"They can't wait five minutes? Come on,
Sarah, just stay for a little while and tell me
about your family. I like your little brother. Do
you have any big ones I should worry about?"

Sarah sighed and dutifully recited the list of
Mausts. "There are Peter and Daniel, older
than me. They are sons of my father's first wife
who died in childbirth. Lucas, Ruth, and Jacob
are the younger ones still at home. There now,
you know all about us. I will come back later
for the tray."

With that she turned on the heel of one sensible black shoe and left the room, leaving
Matt sputtering.

"But—but—what about me?" he demanded.

Sarah was already gone. Blossom remained
in the doorway, giving him the evil eye and a
soft woof that set her droopy jowls jiggling.
Then the dog abandoned him too.

Matt sat back against the pillows, thunderstruck. Women just didn't resist him like that.
Lord, had the beating he'd received somehow
knocked the magnetism out of him? There was
a frightening idea. He speared a chunk of roast

beef and popped it in his mouth, chewing thoughtfully.

No, no, he reflected, that wasn't the case at all. Sarah was attracted. He'd seen it in her eyes, tasted it in her kiss. Lord, that sweet kiss! She was scared. She needed a little wooing, that was all. Well, hell, there weren't many better at that than he was, he reflected with typical doctors' arrogance.

He'd start fresh after dinner. He'd go downstairs and just woo the sensible shoes right off her. There was something special about the sparks he felt inside when Sarah was near. They were brighter than any he'd felt recently. They made him feel enthusiastic about life. He wanted to explore that feeling. He wanted to see it reflected in Sarah's eyes. Something deep inside him ached with hunger for it. And he was going to start right after dinner, he thought as the pills kicked in and his eyelids began to pull down like weighted drapes. His fork had dropped over the edge of the bed, and Blossom scampered in from the hall to snatch the meat off the lines.

Right after dinner he'd start his campaign to win Sarah Troyer. Or maybe after he'd had a little nap. . . .

4

Sarah had been working at Thornewood Inn for about two months. She had her own small room on the second floor—adjacent to Matt's, in fact, just on the other side of the bathroom—and she lived at the inn full-time with the exception of every other weekend when Amish church services were held. Then she spent Saturday night and Sunday with her family, who lived just a mile down the road.

John and Ingrid Wood had purchased the big farmhouse outside Jesse nearly a year before and had been slowly, lovingly renovating it, sanding and polishing the old hardwood floors, stripping paint from cupboards, tearing out dropped ceilings and restoring the plasterwork hidden beneath. The end result was a house Sarah thought of as luxurious if perhaps a little overdone for her plain tastes.

Billowing lace curtains hung like froth at the windows. Armchairs and sofas were plump and plentiful, covered in patterned fabrics in shades of rose and ruby and rich hunter green. Framed works of art Ingrid lovingly referred to as "primitives" adorned the fancy papered walls. Thornewood now boasted four guest rooms and three baths with fancy claw-footed tubs.

In Sarah's opinion the best room by far was the library, outfitted with comfortable stuffed chairs and shelves and shelves of books. The painted white shelves were built into the walls and stretched from floor to ceiling on two sides of the room. There were all kinds of books—the travel books John Wood had written, encyclopedias, novels, history books, current magazines on world events, cooking, and fashion. Easily her favorite part of her job was spending her spare moments in the library soaking up the printed words like a human sponge.

For as long as she could remember she had loved books. Even before she could read them she had carried them around and looked at the pictures and stared at the words, loving the look of them. Learning to read had seemed the most wonderful, magical thing in the world to her, and she had never understood other children who found it a tedious chore. Reading had opened up the world to her. It was the one thing that could transport her away from the dullness of farm life. There weren't so many books to be had at the little Amish country school she had attended, and they were scarce around the Maust household, but at the age of eight Sarah had wandered away from her mother, who had been shopping for canning supplies, and into the Jesse public library. The librarian had granted her permission to check out books, and her life had not been the same since.

Her father had disapproved of her excessive reading, and she had spent much of her youth sneaking away when she could to read in her grandmother's attic. Isaac said it was books that had put so many foolish ideas in her head. He blamed books for Sarah's overactive imagination and for her yearnings. Sarah knew that the yearnings had always been there inside her. Books had made it possible for her to satisfy some of those longings vicariously. Books had probably saved her from committing more rash, reckless acts than she actually had done, but there was no use telling her father that.

At any rate, it was books not people she turned to when she was feeling lonely or restless or troubled. And so it was to the library she went when the last of her work was done on the fourth day of Matt Thorne's stay at Thornewood Inn. She took off her shoes and her *kapp* and curled up in her favorite chair, surrounded by books, seeking some solace for the disquiet in her soul.

None came. And it wasn't the fault of the books or her job. Again and again her thoughts turned to the man sleeping upstairs. She had done her best to avoid him during the past two days, rushing into his room when he rang his bell and rushing back out as soon as she'd seen to whatever his need had been, but it hadn't put an end to the desires stirring inside her—the desire to be near him, to touch him, to listen to him speak, even if it was just to complain about the boredom of being confined to bed.

She closed her eyes and bit her lip, a low, helpless sound forming in her throat. She clutched the big encyclopedia to her chest and wished with all her heart that some answer would seep out of it and soak into her, but that didn't happen. The only thing that filled her head was the image of Matt Thorne, looking at her, studying her as if she were an intricate puzzle to solve, smiling at her with his crooked boyish grin, kissing her.

Oh, Lord, it had been so long since she'd been kissed, not since Samuel had died. Guilt nipped at her as she admitted her husband had never generated the kind of sparks Matt had. Samuel had been a good man, a good friend, but what had passed between them as husband and wife had never been passionate.

For a long time Sarah had blamed herself for wanting passion. She had been raised to believe in a woman's duty to her husband and to God, that the act of joining with a man was for but one purpose—to create life. And still her heart had ached for something more.

Maybe her father had been right in that respect. If not for her reading she would never have known that people outside her sect expected something grander of love than duty. In her community marriage was most often based on friendship and compatibility and the desire, the need, for children. But in her heart she ached for something more.

Now she found herself caught in the no-man's-land between two cultures. An Amish woman doing an English job. The English thought of her as purely plainly Amish. Her own people saw her as a rebel and shook their heads and muttered prayers under their breath. She was an Amish woman in dress and speech and manner. But in her heart she ached for something more.

And what she ached for most just now was the touch of Matt Thorne. Sin that it was, she couldn't stop wanting it.

Heaven above, what had she started by giving in to her need to have a little adventure?

Matt stopped outside the door to the library and stood quietly in the darkened hall for a long moment. He'd awakened from his latest "little nap" at eleven-thirty, disgusted with himself for losing yet another chance to charm Sarah. He had figured she would certainly be sound asleep by now, while he, with a completely goofed-up internal clock, was wide awake and starving for food and companionship. Thinking he could at least find the former downstairs in the kitchen, he had pulled on a pair of sweatpants and made his way down the stairs as quietly as a man with a cane could. The puddle of light spilling out of the library had drawn his attention and he'd gone down the hall without managing to alert either Sarah or Blossom the Wonder Hound.

He stood now watching her, studying her like he might study a work of art, watching the play of light on her features, looking for the secret meaning to her expression and pose. She sat curled on the dark green sofa, embracing a book as a child might embrace a teddy bear, her eyes squeezed tight in concentration on a thought that would doubtless remain a mystery to him.

Lord, she was lovely. So simple, so pretty. He'd been watching her now for four days and he couldn't get over her mixture of innocence and hidden fire, the sweetness of her smile and the bright curiosity in her eyes. He didn't feel worthy of touching her, but at the same time it was what he most wanted to do. He wanted to hold her as she was holding her book and have some of that simple purity wash away the dark edges of his soul. Hell, he just plain wanted her. He was at one of life's great crossroads, and at the moment the only path he wanted to follow was the one that led across his sister's library to Sarah Troyer. He didn't question the urge; he merely gave in to it, being a man used to having his own way.

"Doing a little light reading, I see," he said dryly.

Sarah jolted out of her meditation, her eyes widening, her heart racing from something more than just the start he'd given her. He stood before her looking rumpled and irresistible in soft-looking baggy gray trousers and wool socks that fell around his ankles. He was eyeing the stacks of books she'd placed around her with amusement. There had to be thirty of them, all sizes and types, piled in groups of four and five on the arm and seat of the sofa and on the floor in front of her. If she'd sat in that chair for a week, she wouldn't have been able to read them all.

"You shouldn't be out of bed." It was the first thing that came to her mind and she cringed inwardly, wondering if she was thinking of his welfare or her own.

Matt decided it was a rhetorical comment and made no reply as he eased himself down on the middle cushion of the sofa. He plucked the encyclopedia out of Sarah's hands and glanced over the page she'd had it opened to. "I guess a person can never know too much about the manufacture of ball bearings. I haven't kept up with it myself. My ideas are probably horribly out of date."

Sarah pulled the book out of his hands and closed it, her mouth twisting into a wry little smile.

"Ah, a smile. Does that mean you're not still mad at me?"

"I wasn't angry with you. Why would you think I was?"

Matt lifted his arms in an exaggerated shrug. "Oh, I don't know. I guess the last time a woman shot daggers at me with her eyes, largely refused to speak with me for two days, and ran out of my room at the first opportunity, she was angry with me. Something about my lack of charm."

"I can't imagine that," Sarah muttered dryly.

"Really?" He grinned engagingly. "You find me charming? Even in my current state of dishabille?"

Sarah fidgeted, picking at the wrinkles she'd pressed into her dress with books, uncomfortable with his line of questioning. "I don't find you . . . anything. You're Ingrid's brother. A guest here."

"Mmmm . . . I see," he murmured, nodding doctor-style. "I take it you enjoy reading," he said, fingering through the pile nearest him. A collection of Mark Twain, a book on restoring Victorian homes, a hefty tome on the Civil War.

Sarah stroked her hand over the big book in her lap the way she might stroke a cat, absently, lovingly. "I love to read and to learn," she admitted quietly. "I read all I can about everything."

She loved to learn even though she had been given only a minimal education. Matt thought of the inner-city kids he had dealt with, the opportunities for education that were handed them courtesy of the taxpayers, and which they casually, disdainfully tossed aside in favor of making money selling dope and stealing cars. He imagined what Sarah could have done, given their opportunities.

"Did you ever think of going to college?" he asked.

Think of it? She had dreamed of it constantly as a teenager, but the dream had been well beyond her reach. "I couldn't," was all she said.

"Your people don't believe in encouraging bright young minds?"

The remark hurt, regardless of her own private opinions. She shot Matt an angry look. "My place was on the farm. We are farmers and carpenters and wives of farmers and carpenters. What sense would there be in spending money on fancy schools?"

"None, I guess," Matt replied softly. Her answer sounded like a line she had memorized out of a book of Amish philosophy. He had the distinct feeling it was not her own. No one with such a desire to learn could have subscribed to such an idea. But he didn't push the issue.

He picked up her *kapp* and examined its sheer fine mesh, the careful workmanship, the delicate ties. She stared at it, too, with a look that was akin to horror, as if she'd just realized she'd been sitting there half-naked. Her hand went self-consciously to her hair. Impulsively, Matt reached up and covered her nervous hand with his own, overlapping it so that his fingertips stroked the crown of her head. He got the impression that she would have sunk down into the netherworld of the sofa with the lint and cracker crumbs and loose change if she could have.

"You have very pretty hair," he said softly. It had the texture and sheen of sable, and there were masses of it wound and pinned and knotted at the back of her head. It nearly took his breath away to imagine what it must look like down. "Why do you hide it?"

"It is the way of my people. A woman's hair is her glory and only for her husband to see, else it would be *Hochmut*, pride. Pride is a sin."

"I think the sin is in hiding away something so lovely."

Sarah herself had long wanted to go with her hair loose and flowing for the wind to

tease and tangle. She associated the sensation
with freedom of spirit. But it irked her that she
wanted to agree with this outsider who was already so dangerous to her, so she answered
with one of her father's most famous infuriat-
ing lines. "It's the way of our people, not for
you to agree or disagree. It's just our way."

"Well, it's not mine," Matt said pleasantly,
smiling when she scowled and batted his hand
away from the pins that were holding her bun
in place. He slouched against the cushions, letting his arm fall along the curve of the back of
the couch. "And I have a feeling it wouldn't be
the way of an expert tree climber either."

Sarah shuddered at the thought of him reading her mind so easily. "I was a little girl then.
Now I'm a woman."

"I noticed, believe me," Matt said dryly. "In
spite of the lengths you go to, to hide the fact,
I noticed."

"Again you make fun," Sarah snapped, deliberately taking offense. It seemed safer to
keep him at an arm's length with bad temper,
so she dredged up all she had. She vaulted out
of her seat to pace the floor, knocking over a
stack of books in the process. "Always with
your teasing and cracking wise, making fun."

"No!" Matt protested, pushing himself to his
feet. Dizziness swam through his head but he
couldn't decide whether it was from his condi-

tion or from the sucker punch Sarah had just delivered.

"A kiss and a pinch and make sport of the little Amish maid—"

"Wait a minute!" He grabbed her shoulders, effectively halting her pacing if not her tirade.

"Just because I wear simple clothes and live a simple life doesn't mean I'm simpleminded, Matt Thorne," she declared, glaring into his face.

"I never said you were. I never implied you were. Jeez, Sarah, this isn't the Victorian Age. I'm not the kind of man who goes around tumbling housemaids for a cheap thrill."

"What do you want from me then?" It wasn't a safe question to ask. No matter what his answer was, she would be caught. If he said he wanted something, she couldn't give it and face her family. If he said he wanted nothing . . . She didn't want to think of what that would mean to her even though it was what was best.

Matt gave her a tender look. "How about a little friendship, for starters?"

Now what was she supposed to do? Her plan had been to scare him away with her bad temper and righteous indignation. And he was asking her to be his friend. The idea was much too appealing, much too tempting.

"I'm sorry if you took my remarks the wrong

way, Sarah. I was only teasing. I didn't mean to hurt your feelings. I'd never do that."

The gentleness in his voice was her undoing. She couldn't stand the idea that she'd hurt him. So much for her impromptu strategy.

"No," she murmured, looking down at the nubby toes of his wool socks. "I'm sorry. I shouldn't have snapped at you. What kind of hostess I make, taking my temper out on the guests?"

"You make a fine hostess," Matt said, just barely resisting the urge to draw her up against him and hold her. Instead, he crooked a finger under her chin and tilted her head back so he could lose himself in the endless depths of her lake-blue eyes.

Sarah stared up at him, afraid that he would see every feeling she was struggling with, and equally afraid that he wouldn't. She thought for one heart-stopping instant that he was going to kiss her again, but he gave her a tender smile instead.

"You've had a rough day, you're tense. I know just the thing to fix that."

"You do?" A number of half-formed notions tried to weave their way through the sensual fog in her mind, notions that involved lips and skin and strength and softness and whispered words. None of them quite got a hold, though, and Matt backed away from her, leaving her feeling abandoned.

He went to the bookshelves, to John Wood's fancy radio-stereo machine, which she had always been afraid to touch. With a flick of a switch and a twist of a knob, soft music filled the room. Sarah shivered a little at the magic of it and at the unfamiliar beauty of it. She was used to music; she had grown up in a house filled with singing. But always the Amish songs were about love to God and duty and suffering gladly and going to heaven at the end of a long, painful life. English music was about the world and the relationships between people. It seemed to her, in the little bit she'd heard, that most of it was about love. Falling in love, falling out of love, the glory of love, the pain of love. The one playing now was sung by a man with a strong, smoky voice crooning that he'd be in trouble if she left him now.

"Paul Young," Matt murmured appreciatively, returning to stand in front of her again. A relaxed smile curved his wide, handsome mouth as he took a deep cleansing breath and sighed. "Music to get mellow by. Take a deep breath and let it out slowly."

Sarah did as instructed, letting the air hiss out of her lungs slowly only to suck in a sharp breath when Matt settled his hands on her shoulders. He clucked his tongue in reproof, but his eyes were twinkling and Sarah couldn't decide whether he was being serious or not. He made her feel so emotionally off balance, a

part of her—the coward in her—wanted to run
out of the room and upstairs to the safe haven
of her quarters, but another part of her was
too drawn to him, too intrigued by him, too
tempted. She took another deep breath and expelled it.

"I'm afraid I'm not up to playing Patrick
Swayze," Matt said. "So dancing is out."

"Who is this Patrick? A friend of yours?"

"Not exactly," Matt said with a chuckle. Half
the women in the free world would have given
their fingernails to dance with Patrick Swayze;
Sarah didn't even know who he was. Of course
she wouldn't. She had probably never been to
see a movie. He thought for a minute what it
would be like to take her to her first. It would
be like experiencing it for the first time himself all over again. Everything would be that
way with Sarah. Her innocence would make
the world seem new. Lord, how tempting that
was to a man who'd seen too much of the
worst of it.

"Never mind," he said at last. "Anyway, the
point here is to get you to relax."

"I am relaxed."

"Fibber." His fingers massaged her shoulders in a slow, sensuous rhythm. "Close your
eyes and just listen to the music, let yourself
sway with it."

Sarah did as she was told and was filled by
a strange feeling. It was a little like being un-

derwater, she thought. She was drifting in a
sea of sound, weightless, boneless, sightless.
The only thing anchoring her to reality were
Matt's hands, hands she began fantasizing
about working magic on other parts of her.

"Mmm . . . that's it," Matt whispered.

His voice washed over her in the same kind
of sensual wave as the music, warm and soft.
The Paul Young song ended and another began with no interruption between the two.
This song was even slower, softer, more heart
wrenching. The words seemed to reach right
into her to touch her soul. It was another song
about needing love, about hungering for love,
a prayer for God to speed the love of a special
someone to the singer.

Matt listened to the stirring strains of "Unchained Melody" and watched the look of
sweet yearning that came over Sarah's face,
and felt something melt inside him. The city,
the ER, the noise, the violence were a million
miles away in that instant, and he was glad. It
was just the two of them and the beginning of
something special. He didn't know where this
growing feeling would take them, but he
wanted to find out.

It seemed the most natural thing in the
world for him to step closer to her, to take her
in his arms. He couldn't think why he had resisted the urge this long. He was a man accustomed to getting what he wanted and what he

wanted was to feel Sarah next to him. It didn't matter that he'd only just met her. He felt like he'd been waiting half his life to find her. Sarah with her funny moods and Mona Lisa smile, her sweetness there to take all the bitterness from him.

He pulled her gently against him as the song built to its soulful crescendo, and felt the most incredible sense of rightness and peace. It felt so good, it ached inside him. He brushed his lips against her temple, kissing the fragile skin, his breath stirring the baby-fine tendrils of hair that curled there like wisps of silk.

As the last strains of the melody drifted away Sarah stepped back and looked up at him, her eyes so dark a blue, they looked the color of pansies. She stared up at him a long moment, saying nothing, her expression carefully blank.

"Sarah." He didn't know what he meant to say. All that came out was her name, as soft as a secret.

"I . . . I'd best say good night," she whispered, backing slowly away from him, the way she would from a dangerous animal encountered in the wild.

He stayed where he was, watching her go, saying nothing. Then she was in the comforting dark of the hall. She curbed the urge to run. By the time she got to the stairs, she stopped altogether, her hands clutching the polished oak newel post as if it were the only thing keeping her from sinking into bedlam.

"Oh, dear heaven," she whispered, her voice trembling with emotion. "Please don't let this happen. Please don't let me fall in love with him."

But as she climbed the stairs to her room, she had the terrible feeling it was already too late for prayers.

5

It seemed like the wisest course of action was to distance herself from Matt as much as she could. Sarah had come to this conclusion during the course of another long, sleepless night. He wouldn't be staying forever. If she could just manage to keep her heart out of reach until he had gone back to the city, maybe it wouldn't hurt so much when he left.

Her taste for adventure had been seriously depleted by her fear of pain. Adventure probably wasn't all it was cracked up to be anyway, she told herself as she readied a tray of warm muffins and fresh fruit for Matt's breakfast. So far this one had mostly just upset her.

Her thoughts strayed to the memory of being held in Matt's arms and swaying against him as an unseen person in the background sang out all the yearning that had ever been in her heart.

Yes, that had been a sweet moment. And the kiss. That had been precious to her as well. But the risk here was so great and the chance of happiness so small. She had to be realistic about it. Matt was a good man, but there was no future in letting herself fall in love with him. She just had to accept that fact. If she still wanted an adventure, she could try something safer, like figuring out how to make brownies in the microwave oven. Plenty of challenge there, and the only risk was exploding brownie mix all over the kitchen. Or she could have another go at running the VCR. Now there was a real adventure. Every time she tried to put in one of the cartridges Ingrid had told her contained movies, the thing spat it right back out at her. She'd tried touching various buttons, but it only blinked and beeped at her and now the clock would do nothing but flash 12:00—12:00—12:00, and she was terrified she'd ruined it.

Yes, mastering electronic appliances was an adventure that was more her speed. Adventures of the heart were out of her league. Now if she could just get Matt to take the hint.

She wrote him a note telling him she was going into town and stuck it among the muffins. She was hoping he would still be asleep so she could just leave the tray inside his door and slip away from the house before he had a chance to interfere with her plan. There were errands that had to be run in preparation for the guests that would be arriving later in the day. She figured it would take her all morning at the very least to take care of them. That seemed like a good start on escaping the magnetic charm of Dr. Thorne.

She crept up the stairs, taking great care not to rattle the china or slosh the juice. The aroma of coffee wafted up into her face from the thermal carafe, and her stomach rumbled loudly, reminding her that she hadn't taken any time to feed herself yet today. She shushed it and tiptoed down the hall, creeping along the wall to avoid the squeaky spot in the floor. Blossom shuffled along behind her making snuffling noises, trailing the scent of blueberry muffins.

Cradling the tray against her, Sarah managed to work one hand free to grasp the knob on the door to Matt's room. With excruciating patience she turned it a fraction of an inch at a time so as not to make any noise. She pushed the door open a bare inch, then two. Then Blossom butted it wide open with her nose and went bounding in, howling, long ears waving like flags. The basset hound hurled herself at the feet of Matt Thorne, who stood dead center in the room, naked as the day he was born.

"Oh, *mein Gott!*" Sarah exclaimed on a shocked gasp. Her fingers went instantly numb and the breakfast tray made a noisy trip to the floor. Orange juice spewed across the hardwood. Muffins went bouncing in all directions with Blossom chasing after them, trying to catch them in her mouth like balls.

Matt stayed where he was, too enchanted by the sight of a grown woman turning purple with embarrassment to worry about his unclothed state. Sarah dropped to her knees and glued her gaze to the floor as she fumbled with the scattered contents of the tray. Silver rattled against china. The tightly capped coffee thermos slipped out of her grasp and rolled across the floor like a bowling pin.

"I'm so sorry," she mumbled. "I should have knocked. I thought you would still be asleep. I had no idea you'd be . . . be—"

"Naked," Matt supplied, amusement twitching his lips.

"Oh, *mein Gott*."

It didn't matter that she was no longer looking at him. She'd already gotten an eyeful and all of it was burned into her brain. She'd seen him with his shirt off and she'd seen him in his running shorts, but what she'd just seen certainly made a big impression on her overall view of the man. She squeezed her eyes shut, trying to banish the image from her mind and only succeeded in calling up every detail in startling clarity. Trim hips, muscular thighs. Flat belly with a line of dark hair leading down the center from the edge of his bandages to spread into a thicket of curls around that which made him male—extremely male. "Oh, *mein Gott*," she mumbled in despair.

"Gee, Sarah, I think that's enough praise. I'll get a big head . . . or something," Matt said, barely able to contain his chuckles. He grabbed his bath towel off the end of the bed and slung it around his hips out of deference for her delicate sensibilities and to disguise the fact that he was enjoying having her see him just a little too much. "It's okay, honey, really. I'm decent now."

She chanced a peek up at him and went crimson all over again. Decent? Decadent was more like it. The man had no sense of propriety. He certainly had other fine attributes, she thought with a flash of heat in her face, but modesty was not among them.

Matt dropped another towel on the floor to sop up juice and knelt on a dry spot, bending over to look into Sarah's face.

"Sweetheart, it's okay. It's no big deal. I don't mind you seeing my body. We've all got one under our clothes."

She looked at him, utterly shocked, and sputtered, "I don't got one and you had ought to keep yours covered! It looks like a very big deal to me!"

She shoved her soggy note at him and fled, leaving the tray behind. Matt fell over on the floor, laughing and groaning, holding his aching ribs, finally howling in a combination of hysteria and pain. Blossom dropped the muffin she was devouring and howled along.

Sarah grabbed her cloak and bonnet and rushed out the back door of the house. Gravel scuffed her shoes as she ran across the driveway and down to the small barn where the Woods allowed her to keep her horse. Her breath fogged in the crisp fall air like steam. It probably *was* steam, she thought. Everything inside her felt hot and churning.

Why had she had to see Matt that way after making her big decision to end the adventure of getting to know him? Now everything female in her just wanted to get to know him better. Lust. Pure, sinful lust, that was what it was. And to her discredit, she didn't feel the least bit ashamed of it. What she felt was angry and frustrated.

She grabbed a section of harness and tossed it on Otis without taking the time to brush him first. She had kept the brown gelding for herself when she had sold the rest of the farm and equipment after Samuel's death. The horse looked at her now with his limpid brown eyes, blinking as if she had just awakened him from a deep, restful sleep.

"We're going to town," she told him, buckling the bellyband with more force than usual, winning herself a fierce offended look from

the old horse. She ignored him, too wrapped
up in the whirlwind of her own emotions.

She would go to town and do her errands as
slowly as she could, lingering over each task.
And when they were all accomplished, she
would think up some more. She would invent
reasons to stay in town until she absolutely
had to return to the inn in order to greet the
weekend guests. She would be safe then, surrounded by nosy, demanding tourists. She
would cocoon herself with their presence and
shut out Matt Thorne as much as she could.
Maybe by doing all that she would be able to
forget about how wonderfully male he looked
and how her body had never experienced any
kind of sexual satisfaction.

She slipped the horses's bridle on and led
him out into the yard where her buggy was
parked. Otis demonstrated his lack of enthusiasm for his work by moving as slowly as he
could, stretching out his long neck as he was
pulled along, backing up between the shafts of
the buggy one plodding step at a time. Sarah
tried to rush him, but in a contest between a
hundred-and-twenty-pound woman and a
thousand-pound horse there was likely to be
only one outcome. She hurried where she
could, fastening the tugs and buckling the
back bands with the speed acquired through
hundreds of harnessings. The closer she came
to finishing and the nearer she felt to freedom,

the faster she moved. Just another two minutes and she would be on the road, alone with her confounded lust, leaving Matt Thorne behind to think what he would.

He probably thought she was a fool. A foolish, prudish, backward yokel. He was probably amused by her lack of sophistication. Heaven knew, he no doubt had a flock of slick, polished city women waiting for him back in Minneapolis, none of whom would run away from seeing him naked.

"I wouldn't have either," she muttered. "Except that . . ."

Except what? She had a duty to her family and her faith? No, that wasn't what had made her run.

"Mind if I tag along?"

Sarah's hands stilled on the harness. She barely resisted the urge to close her eyes and fall against Otis in a swoon of despair. Another two minutes and she would have been gone. Just two more minutes.

"Does groaning between your teeth that way mean yes in Amish?"

She turned and scowled at Matt, half-expecting to see him standing there with a blush-pink towel swathing his hips. He was dressed. Actually, he looked more respectable than she'd ever seen him. He wore baggy tweed trousers, a blue shirt, and a black leather jacket to cut the chill of the October

morning. His hair was combed and still damp
from a washing. The gleam in his dark eyes
was pure mischief.

"You ought to be in bed."

Matt grinned and moved a step closer. "You
certainly have a burning desire to see me between the sheets, Blue Eyes. I would have been
more than willing to discuss the issue with you
a while ago, but since I've gone to all the trouble of putting on clothes . . ."

"You're shameless," Sarah grumbled, snapping a rein to her gelding's bit.

"I hate to be immodest," Matt said, "but I
don't think I have anything to be ashamed of.
Do you?"

The pink crept back into her cheeks as the
picture of him flashed again in her mind. He
was a beautifully made man. He certainly
didn't have anything to be ashamed of.

"Come on, sweetheart," he said cajolingly,
stepping a little closer and gently taking hold
of her arm. He turned her toward him, but she
refused to look at him. "You were a married
lady. You've seen a naked man before."

"That was different." Lord, please don't let
him ask how different, she thought. As different as day and night. She had scarcely seen
Samuel completely undressed and when she
had, she hadn't been inspired to feel the wild
emotions that had careened around inside her
when she'd seen Matt. Guilt pressed down on

her, but she shooed it away. It wasn't her fault Samuel had been slight of build and Matt Thorne was . . . not.

"I'm sorry I laughed," Matt whispered, his breath fanning her ear, his voice an almost-tangible caress to her senses. His fingers were gentle on her arm, stroking lightly through the fabric of her black cape. "You were just so cute all flabbergasted."

Sarah wasn't sure how to respond, if she was expected to respond at all. Flattery was a foreign concept to her. She stepped back from the horse and out of Matt's grasp, deciding that to dismiss the topic was probably the smartest thing she could do. "Are you sure you are up to riding? It's three miles to town."

Matt eyed the boxy black buggy and the old horse hitched to it. It wouldn't have been his transportation of choice, but if it meant getting to sit beside Sarah, looking at her and smelling the clean soap-scent of her, and possibly brushing up against her every now and again, he was willing to settle.

"I can handle it. Too bad Ingrid didn't arrange to have my car brought down," he said, helping Sarah up into the buggy. "It's a Jag," he added proudly.

"What's a Jag?"

He eased him self onto the thinly padded bench seat, staring at her incredulously. "What's a Jag? A Jaguar XJ6. Only one of the finest automobiles known to man. Leather interior, digital CD player, all-aluminum fuel-injected four-liter twenty-four valve inline-six. Two hundred and twenty-three horses under the hood."

There. Let her scoff at that, Matt thought. Women never failed to be impressed by his car, even if they didn't know what he was talking about. They always had sense enough to know all that jargon meant great things.

Sarah gave him a crooked little smile that clearly said she thought he was one brick short of a full load. She slapped the reins against the gelding's back and said, "Two hundred and twenty-three horses? One has always done just fine for me."

"Very funny." He reached into his hip pocket and pulled his wallet out. "I have a picture of it. Want to see?"

She arched a brow in disbelief. "You carry a photograph of your car?"

"Well . . . sure," he said defensively, pouting a little.

Sarah gave him a long, amused look and burst into laughter.

The ride into Jesse was surprisingly pleasant for them both. Sarah's embarrassment subsided and she relaxed enough to enjoy Matt's company. He was nothing short of gentlemanly, chatting with her about her family, asking questions about the horse and buggy and listening with genuine interest as she told him about the quiet simplicity of Amish life. She pointed out the farms of family friends—Jon Schrock the carpenter, Jake Yoder and his wife, Katie, who made beautiful baskets and sold them in Jesse at the folk-art center. She told him the names of the big Belgian horses Martin Lapp was working through his cornfield.

For Matt the ride was one of his first forays into fresh air and sunshine since his hospitalization. He felt much better than he had the day before. He especially felt better since he was near Sarah, and he decided she was a much greater tonic than any medication he had been prescribed.

He listened to her describe her people and her way of life, so very different from the life he was used to, slower and so peaceful. He watched the way she handled the reins, her small, unadorned hands sure and steady. She was dressed in what he had come to think of as her "uniform"—heavy dark hose, black shoes, blue dress with a black "cape" or bodice covering, and apron pinned in place. Over this she had put a heavy black woolen cloak that tied at the throat. Instead of the small white cap he had grown used to seeing on her, she wore a larger, more concealing black bonnet, the brim of which hid most of her profile like the blinkers on Otis's bridle. It was garb he might have found quaint on some anonymous Amish woman. On Sarah he found it annoying. He wanted to see more of her. She was a lovely young woman. It was frustrating to only catch glimpses of that loveliness.

He tried to picture her in his mind's eye in jeans and a sweatshirt, but he couldn't do it. He could see her in a flowing flowered skirt and a dainty blouse with a lace collar. Something feminine and pretty with her hair tumbling in a thick, magnificent wave down her back. Yes, he thought with a smile, he could picture that quite easily, almost as easily as he could picture her wearing nothing at all.

He sat back and enjoyed the ride, enjoyed the scenery, enjoyed the quiet of the countryside. It had bothered him his first couple of days here. He was used to the noise of a busy city. But now, as he sat relaxed beside Sarah, he absorbed the peace of it. A cornfield stood on one side of the road, tall beige stalks dry and ready for picking. On the other side cattle grazed in a tree-dotted pasture, the trees in full fall color. It was beautiful rolling countryside. So peaceful, so far removed from the gritty reality of the inner city. There were no gang wars here, no endless parade of junkies and bums and drunks. There was still order and sanity in a place like Jesse.

In all fairness, there was still order and san-

ity in most of the Twin Cities area too. The
level of urban squalor wasn't nearly so de-
pressing as it was in most cities, but the de-
cline in the poorer areas was steady and
disheartening and spreading slowly into the
near suburbs like creeping rot. In most respects the metropolitan area was a great place
to live—clean, pretty, culturally active, artisti-
cally aware—and most of its inhabitants probably didn't give much thought to the prospects
of decay and rising crime rates and crumbling
morality, but these were things Matt saw on a
daily basis. Knowing all those problems were
not just a couple hundred miles away from
Jesse, but a whole state of mind away, was a
relief for him.

The town of Jesse looked like something out
of Norman Rockwell's imagination, tree-lined
streets and prominent church steeples, brick
shop-fronts and tubs of chrysanthemums on
the street corners. A tour bus was unloading in
front of the chamber of commerce building,
and tourists turned with cameras in hand to
snap photos of Sarah's horse and buggy.

"You're a celebrity," Matt said with a grin.

"I'm an oddity." There was a bitterness in
her voice she didn't usually feel, and she realized that while she didn't much care what the
tourists thought of her, she suddenly cared
very much that Matt Thorne not think of her
as a curiosity. He didn't say anything, poor

man. What could he say? Of course she was an oddity to him. He was a hotshot doctor from the big city. It was a sure bet his life was not crowded with Amish.

"I have to go to the drugstore and the fabric shop and to the grocer's and the dime store," she said, pulling off onto a side street and up to an honest-to-goodness hitching rail.

Matt was amazed. A town with hitching rails! He hadn't imagined anything like it existed except on reruns of *Gunsmoke*. Sarah, of course, didn't think it strange at all. She wasn't the oddity here, he thought, he was. He was the alien invading her territory and so were the tourists.

"Is there anyplace in particular you'd like to go?" she asked.

"Ah, well, I thought I'd pay a call on the local doctor, get my dressing changed, have him pull the stitches out of my chin, talk shop."

"The ride didn't injure you, did it?" Sarah asked, turning her face up to him. Her eyes looked even bigger, widened by concern and framed by the stiff brim of her bonnet.

Matt felt a little bubble of warmth in his chest. He smiled at her and reached a finger out to skim down her nose. He was pretty sure the buggy ride had jarred his teeth loose, but Otis wasn't going to be able to drag that information out of him, not when Sarah was looking up at him that way. "No. I'm fine. Thanks for asking."

"Sure," she said, giving him her teasing smile. "That's just my way of seeing if you're fit to help carry the grocery bags."

They both chuckled at that, then time just caught and held, frozen in the air like a snowflake as their gazes met.

I wish he would kiss me again, Sarah thought, knowing she shouldn't want it, but wanting it just the same.

I want to lean down and kiss her, Matt thought, the magnetic force of desire tugging at him, pulling him a fraction of an inch closer as his gaze focused on the vulnerable curve of her mouth. He wanted to taste her again, her sweetness, her innocence. Then a gaggle of tourists rounded the corner, cackling and waddling along the sidewalk like a band of roaming geese, and the moment was gone.

They agreed on a time to meet back at the buggy. Sarah pointed Matt toward Dr. Coswell's office, then went her own way.

At the fabric shop she purchased sturdy blue cloth to make two new shirts for Jacob because it seemed he was growing faster than her mother could sew for him and because she simply enjoyed doing it. Doing things for Jacob helped to ease the ache of not having children of her own.

As usual, her gaze wandered longingly over the array of patterned fabrics that crowded the displays of the small shop and she thought of

how she might look in an English-style skirt
cut from the bolt of cream with large mauve
roses and dark green leaves on it. She ran her
fingers over the nubby texture of a fine white
eyelet and pictured it as a flowing nightgown
adorned with pale blue ribbons. But she
bought only her length of durable broadcloth
and moved on to the next of her errands.

As she went about her business she did her
best to ignore the curious looks and the out-
right stares directed at her by other patrons of
the businesses, mainly people from out of
town, for the townsfolk of Jesse had long ago
become accustomed to seeing Plain people.
Still, it made her uncomfortable. More so today than most days. Today she didn't want to
feel so different from everyone else. Today she
didn't want to have it pointed out to her that
she wasn't just an ordinary woman doing her
shopping. Today everything about her Amishness irritated her like burlap chafing against
her skin. She wanted to fling her bonnet off
and wear sneakers and not worry about her
long skirts snagging on store shelves. And the
reason was Matt Thorne.

At the drugstore she finally gave in. Along
with the supplies for the inn she purchased a
tiny blue vial of perfume called *Evening in
Paris* and a copy of *Glamour* magazine that
featured articles on fall fashions and dating in
the nineties. The clerk gave her a curious look,

but evidently decided all the items were for someone else at Thornewood and made no comment. Sarah paid the bill at the pharmacy counter and quietly thanked the woman. On her way to the front of the store she paused when she was out of view of the clerk and dug her two prizes out of the bag. The perfume she tucked into a small pocket she'd sewn inside the waistband of her apron. The magazine was tucked between the folds of the latest edition of the *Jesse Herald-Dispatch*.

She pressed her packages against her with one arm and arranged the newspaper-magazine combination in her hands, the magazine opened to an ad for ladies' razors. She bumped the drugstore door open with her hip and stepped out onto the sidewalk—directly into the path of her father. His gaze was focused on the hardware store farther down the street and he plowed into her unchecked, sending packages, paper, and magazine all flying.

"Sarah!" he said, startled, grabbing her by the shoulders to catch her from falling.

"Pop!" She sounded—and looked, she supposed—more guilty than surprised, and she could have bit her tongue. She was twenty-five, a grown woman, but with Isaac she would ever feel the wayward adolescent.

She pulled out of his grasp and they both bent to gather up the packages. He got hold of the magazine before she could reach it and he scowled at the picture on the front cover—a doe-eyed young woman with short, wild hair, exaggerated makeup, and a thick collar of gaudy necklaces. Isaac scowled so hard, it seemed to elongate his lean, lined face and lengthen his scruffy gray beard. Thick, woolly eyebrows drew together in a severe V of disapproval that reached from the rim of his black felt hat to the bridge of his nose. With forced calm, Sarah gathered her other articles and then took the magazine from her father's hands as she straightened.

"I'm just in town to do some shopping for the inn," she said. It was probably as much a sin as an out-and-out lie, but she couldn't help not wanting him to think the worldly book was hers. They'd had the argument too many times for her to go looking for it.

Isaac sniffed, his scowl not lessening. He was no more than an inch or two taller than Sarah, but carried himself so straight and so stiffly, she always had the impression of him towering over her. He straightened his heavy work coat, his broad hands brushing off some of the road dust in a gesture that seemed insultingly symbolic to Sarah.

"Where is the woman who runs the place?" he asked in German. "Is she too good to do the shopping?"

"Ingrid is away at her other place of business," Sarah answered primly in the tongue that was her first language. She had always thought it rude to speak a language in public that others couldn't understand—which was, of course, her father's reason for doing it—but she gave in on the point this time. She was having enough trouble grappling for control of her temper. Ingrid was her friend as well as her employer and she took great exception to her father's dim view of the woman.

"A woman running businesses all over the place," Isaac grumbled. "Where is her husband then? Staying in the same house as you without his wife?"

"John Wood is gone to California." She tried not to flinch even inwardly at the information she was not giving her father. God knew the eruption that would cause. Isaac Maust's rebel daughter staying in a house with a handsome young doctor from the Cities and no one to chaperon. It made her dizzy just thinking about it. Then she remembered with a sudden terrible jolt that Jacob knew all about Matt's presence. Jacob, whom Isaac himself had sent to the inn. Her heart thudded in her chest like a hammer. Before she had a chance to think about it, she pressed on. "Ingrid left me in charge of the guests. Five for the weekend."

"Guests." Isaac spat the word, as if using it for tourists were some defilement of the term.

"And one of them teaching your brother filthy foul language."

"What?"

"Jacob came home the other day saying such words. He got his mouth washed out, I can tell you."

Sarah was as appalled as if Jacob had been her own son and Isaac some stranger bent on disciplining the boy for imagined sins. She couldn't hold back her gasp of outrage or her defense. "Gross? Is that the word?" Isaac turned purple. "That's not bad language! It's just a word the English children say—"

"Reason enough to stop him using it. I have one child among the English already. I have no desire to see another go astray."

Sarah drew back, her lips pressed together in a tight line against the pain. How dare he accuse her of going astray when she had tried so hard to stay among them, when every day she fought her own spirit to stay Amish.

She lifted her chin to a stubborn angle her father had seen too many times. "Yes, I've traded my horse for a fancy car, you know. A . . . a . . . Dagmar," she said, not quite sure if that was the right name or not. It sounded impressive nevertheless.

Her sarcasm brought only another disapproving snort. She could feel her father's steel-blue eyes boring into her. "What is this I hear?"

"Hear?" She swallowed hard. "From who?"

"Micah Hochstetler asked you to go to the Beachys' auction with him and you wouldn't go. He says you're acting high and worldly more and more."

"He goes around saying such things and you wonder why I wouldn't go with him?" She rolled her eyes.

"He is a fine young man, a member of the church with his own farm."

"And you think that's reason enough for me to go around with him?"

"I'm thinking if you married and had children as you were meant to, we'd not live in fear of being visited by the deacon."

"I've done nothing to warrant a visit from the deacon!" Sarah protested, her temper flaring as it always did when she exchanged more than five lines with her father.

He stared meaningfully at the magazine in her arms.

"I have committed no sin," Sarah said stubbornly.

"Excuse me," a third voice intruded with a sharp, sarcastic edge. "Is there a problem here?"

Isaac turned and looked at Matt, the old man's face set like a mask of granite. "None that concerns you," he said stiffly in English and he walked away with his head up and his eyes on the hardware store.

Sarah watched him go, a sour mixture of love and hate rolling inside her.

"Friend of yours?" Matt asked softly.

"No," she said, tears burning the backs of her eyes. "He's my father."

As Sarah shopped for her groceries Matt sat in the buggy tied to the hitching rail at the end of the parking lot. Despite the fact that he felt a thousand percent better than he had the day before, he was still a ways from being back to full strength, and the morning's activities had taken a toll on him. He leaned back against the seat as he watched toddlers play in the park across the street, his thoughts going over his visit with Jesse's resident physician.

The man was an insult to doctors in general and probably a menace to his patients. Phillip Coswell was fiftyish, best described as squat with oily, thinning dark hair, and a fine example of a chainsmoker. He'd asked Matt no less than five times what medication he was on, indicating that he either wasn't paying attention or he had a serious problem with concentration. His main topic of conversation had been the scandalous cost of malpractice insurance and how to milk the most out of the Medicare system. During his time in the waiting room, Matt had heard him insult one female patient and deride another for wasting his time. The poor woman had burst into tears. Matt still couldn't get over the fact that the waiting room had been full. People actually depended on that man for their medical care. It was a terrifying thought.

Sarah came out of the store then and Matt's attention shifted abruptly. She looked pale and tense. He wondered what she and her father had been arguing about, but he didn't feel right asking and she hadn't offered to tell him. He reached out to help her into the buggy and they drove up to the door to have the groceries loaded in. Then they were on their way out of Jesse, past the tourists congregating in front of the Viking Café, past the towering corrugated metal structures that comprised the Jesse Grain Elevator, and out once more into the country.

Sarah made no pretense at small task. She kept her attention riveted to her driving and to her effort to keep from bursting into tears. For once she was glad for the concealing aspect of her bonnet. It effectively hid her face from Matt's scrutiny. She knew he was dying to ask her what the problem was, but she had no desire to tell him. She wasn't even sure she could have told him if she wanted to. Her feelings were all tangled up so that she didn't know if she would ever be able to sort them out. It had to do with love and need and duty and obligation and wanting and being afraid.

Complicating it all was Matt himself with his gentle hands and his come-hither grin. She didn't want to talk to him of all people about the issue of her Amishness, not when he made her want so much, not when she so desperately wanted him not to think of her as Amish, even though she knew that was wrong and stupid. Oh, heaven, what a mess!

Suddenly two big, masculine hands settled over hers on the reins and Otis was being guided off the road, onto the path to a field of soybeans. They were about halfway to Thornewood, precisely in the middle of nowhere, with no one else in sight. The buggy rolled to a stop. Otis hung his head and cocked one hind leg. For a moment the only sounds were the wind in the dried grass and the distant screech of a hunting hawk.

Matt plucked at the strings that tied Sarah's bonnet in place and carefully lifted the hat away, setting it on the seat on the other side of her. "Come here, now," he murmured gathering her against him. "Cry it out, whatever it is."

That was all the encouragement Sarah needed. The last of her strength snapped like a twig and she clung to Matt Thorne and cried her heart out. She cried for what she was and what she could never be. She cried because she wanted her father to love her and she hated herself for it. She cried because her heart was set on Matt Thorne and she had to know she was nothing more than an amusement for him. She cried in sobs that wrenched her soul and twisted her heart.

Matt held her tight against him, ignoring the pain in his ribs. It was nothing compared to what the sound of Sarah crying did to his heart. He found himself wanting to track down her father and punch him in the nose. What could he, what could anyone want to say to sweet, innocent Sarah that would make her cry? Whatever it was, he wanted to somehow take it away. He wanted to soothe her hurt. He wanted to protect her.

He ran a hand over her hair and murmured words of comfort, letting his lips brush the top of her head. Pins fell loose and her hair tumbled freely down her back in glorious waves. Matt tangled his hands in it, lifting it, smoothing it, all the while whispering to her as her sobs faded to soft weeping, then sniffles and ragged breathing. Without letting go of her, he reached in his hip pocket for a handkerchief, he tipped her head back and dabbed at her tears and red nose.

"Better?" he asked.

Sarah nodded, feeling embarrassed and foolish and so very grateful to him. She dodged his steady gaze, staring instead at the big damp patches where her tears had stained his shirt. "Thank you," she murmured, her voice sounding rusty and low. "I'm very sorry—"

"No." Matt pressed an index finger to her lips to silence her apology and tilted her head back again so she had no choice but to look at him. Her long lashes were damp and spiky. Her eyes seemed magnified by the sheen of moisture in them, and so blue they made the autumn sky pale in comparison. "Don't be sorry. You needed to cry. I'm a big advocate of people crying when they need to. I'm thinking about writing a paper on it for the *New England Journal of Medicine*."

"Really?" she said, trying to give him a dry smile that trembled a little too much to work.

"Really. You know what else?"

She shook her head.

"I'm going to kiss you."

Having made the announcement, he went ahead and fulfilled the promise, pressing his palms to her cheeks and bending his head down to hers. Their lips met slowly, softly, with the gentlest pressure. Matt sipped at her as if she were a rare fine wine, tasting and savoring. Her mouth was pliant beneath his, warm and salty with the taste of her tears. He deepened the kiss a degree, changing the angle slightly, pulling her a little closer. She slid her arms up around his neck and her breasts flat-

tened against the solid wall of his chest, sending desire shooting through his veins like
adrenaline. Heat seared him just beneath the
surface of his skin and he deepened the kiss a
little more.

Sarah gasped at the first intrusion of his
tongue, unconsciously taking him deeper into
her mouth, then moaned softly in her throat at
the thrill of the intimacy. Her fingers clutched
his shoulders, slipping against the smooth
black leather of his jacket. She wriggled closer
to him, loving the feel of his body against hers,
loving the scent of him and the taste of him.
She let him explore her mouth, hesitantly
meeting his tongue with her own.

Everything else receded but this. Her inner
turmoil, her family, the temporary aspect of
Matt's presence. The world itself spun away,
leaving just the two of them and this moment
and this kiss.

And then it was over.

Matt drew back slowly, staring at her with a
slightly puzzled expression, as if he'd gotten
something he hadn't expected and wasn't sure
why. His hands sifted through her long hair,
drawing it over her shoulders. The ends fell in
thick curls to brush at her thighs.

"Sweet heaven, you're pretty," he murmured.

Sweet heaven. That was where he had

taken her—to the edge of heaven on earth. And as Sarah took up the reins and guided the horse back onto the road, she wondered if she would ever know what it was to go beyond that edge.

6

Sarah found a million things to do the instant they reached Thornewood. She had to see to the unhitching and care of her horse, unloading and putting away the groceries, double-checking the guest rooms and reservations, preparing the snack of cheeses and grapes and French bread that would be offered to the guests upon their arrival.

Matt suspected she was avoiding him again, having been shaken a little by the kiss they had shared, but he didn't press the issue. Hell, he had been shaken by it as well. Shaken right down to his lifelong bachelor toes. He hadn't come here looking to get knocked for a romantic loop by an innocent young maid like Sarah. He wouldn't have even believed it was possible. He was a mature, experienced man, a man who knew the score, a man who had his life neatly categorized. Now he felt as if the stuffing had been pulled out of all his spiffy little pigeonholes. The sturdy ladder of his priorities had collapsed, and the only sure thing rising out of the dust was his desire for Sarah Troyer.

Pleading a genuine case of fatigue, he left
Sarah to her fussing and went upstairs to
crash. He was asleep the instant he hit the bed,
not even noticing when Blossom nosed her
way into the room and made off with one of
his shoes.

He dreamed about the ER at County General, seeing again the face of the young man
whose knife wound he had patched up not two
months before. A Vice Lord. Matt knew by the
black-and-gold colors and the tattoo of a five-
pointed star on the young man's left bicep. He
had learned to read gang signs and fashions
like a cavalryman must have learned the traits
of the various warring tribes of Plains Indians
in the last century. The young Vice Lord had
been brought in holding his ribs and spitting
up blood. Two gurneys down, a junkie was
rambling incoherently, her mind invaded by
demons conjured by crack. Across the room a
member of a rival gang pulled a gun and
started shouting obscenities. A Disciple by his
blue-and-black uniform and the fact that everything about his attire emphasized the
right—his beret was tilted to the right, his belt
buckle hung loose to the right, his right side
pants pocket was turned inside out. There was
an eruption of violence, an explosion; images
tumbled and swirled, all colored in blood and
accompanied by shouts and screams.

And then he was sitting in a buggy, holding

Sarah and listening to the wind, the silence so abrupt, so absolute it hurt his ears.

Matt blinked himself awake and lay staring up at the ceiling. It didn't take Sigmund Freud to figure that one out, he thought. Sarah was a metaphor representing innocence and purity, a tangible symbol he could hold and protect and control in a way he couldn't begin to do with the raw ideals. They were like smoke, slipping through his frantic grasp, swept away by the fetid winds of urban decay. But Sarah was real, living, shining, sweet.

Well, that was all a nice, neat analytical explanation, wasn't it? Why then did clinical understanding do nothing to dilute his deep need to see her and touch her and hold her? Wanting a woman was nothing new to him, but this was something different, something that went beyond symbolism. He wanted Sarah Troyer with something inside him he had never before encountered. Trying to figure it all out left him dizzier than his concussion had.

From somewhere below came the muffled sound of voices. The guests had arrived, en masse by the sound of it. Matt eased himself out of bed and padded barefoot in his underwear to the bathroom where he splashed cold water on his face and ran a comb through his hair. He pulled on a pair of jeans and a soft loose sweater in shades of black and sapphire, wondering wryly if anyone would mistake him

for a member of the Disciples. After giving up
the search for his errant Loafer, he settled for
beat-up sneakers and headed for the foyer and
the source of the cacophony.

The group looked like the assembled cast of
a farce, Matt thought as he descended the
stairs slowly, having left his cane behind.
There was Sarah in her plain uniform and
bright wide eyes, eager to serve and to please;
a chubby couple in their fifties, outfitted in
color-coordinated tourist garb, complete with
cameras hanging from their necks like giant
pendants; and a woman who looked to be
some kind of aging beauty queen with
unnatural-looking russet hair piled on her
head like cotton candy, enormous sunglasses
perched on her nose, enormous breasts, and a
pile of dead foxes draped around the shoulders
of her trim ivory wool suit.

Blossom sat on Sarah's feet with her ears
perked and her head tilted, staring with quizzi-
cal amazement at the limp hides hanging over
the woman's mountainous chest. The basset
hound's rubbery lips quivered and she issued a
whispered woof, as if she were trying to unob-
trusively gain the attention of the pelts.

"Oh, isn't this just the cutest little ol' place!"
the beauty queen drawled, beaming a smile all
around the front hall, though how she could
see anything through her dark glasses was beyond Matt. She twirled around and gave Sarah

a pat on the cheek. "And aren't you just the cutest thing! A real Amish person. Isn't that clever! Wait'll Tim sees you! He's out in the car right now, tryin' to get the price on pork bellies, but he'll be in directly. Just wait'll he sees how cute you are!"

Sarah gave the woman her Mona Lisa look and said nothing.

Matt felt a fist of tension tighten in his chest.

"Marvin, get a picture," the plump wife ordered, elbowing her husband's belly.

Marvin chewed on the stub of an unlit cigar, grumbling as he lifted his camera and fiddled with the knobs. "Cripes, Peg, all I've been doing all day is taking pictures of Amish." He pronounced Amish with a long *A*. His voice was as gritty as gravel, and he spoke in staccato bursts of words, as if his weight and his smoking had constricted his lungs. "They all look alike. We're going to get home and have two hundred and eighty pictures of the same person."

Peg squeezed her bulldog face into a horrific pinched look, glaring into the end of her husband's zoom lens. "Just do it, Marvin. Just humor me. We're on vacation. We're having fun."

Whether you like it or not, Matt added mentally. He watched in amazement as Marvin backed down the hall so he could focus his oversize lens. Mrs. Marvin sidled up next to

Sarah as she might have to a cigar store
wooden Indian and creased a smile into her
pudgy face. The beauty queen moved into the
picture as well, sweeping her fur from her
shoulders with the drama of a runway model.

Blossom snarled, grabbed a mouthful of
fluffy fox tails, and bolted for the kitchen.
The beauty queen squealed and ran after her.
Marvin, looking at the whole thing through
the distorted view of a two-hundred-twenty-
millimeter telephoto lens, didn't have a
chance. The dog hit him in the ankles, knocking him off balance, and the beauty queen
gave him a shoulder in the midsection as she
ran bent over trying to grab the flying ends of
her fur. Marvin flew backward into the
kitchen door, which obligingly swung back
on its hinges.

They ended up in a heap on the polished linoleum, Marvin with the fox stole draped
across his face and Miss Alabama 1967
sprawled unceremoniously over his belly. Blossom took one look at the scene and made a
hasty escape through the doggy hatch in the
back door.

"Oh, Mrs. Parker, Mr. Morton, I'm so sorry!"
Sarah held out a hand to help Mrs. Parker up.
The woman teetered upright on her spike
heels, her tight ivory wool skirt hiked up above
her knees, her nest of russet hair tilting drunkenly, her sunglasses askew. She clutched her

patchwork of fox hides to her chest like a security blanket.

"I'd best go up to my room and repair myself," she said dazedly. "Tim just hates to see me disheveled."

As she staggered out into the hall, Marvin Morton struggled to sit up, cradling his precious camera in his big sausage fingers. "I oughta sue," he said around the crumpled remains of his cigar stub. "I think I've got a whiplash."

"Lucky I'm here then, isn't it?" Matt said coming to stand behind Sarah.

"Why?" he asked, struggling to rise. "Are you a lawyer?"

"No, I'm a doctor. I can examine you and give you a diagnosis and treatment. You're not afraid of big needles, are you? The best thing for whiplash is major doses of cortisone," he said with a perfectly straight face. "Of course, that's excruciating painful in itself."

Marvin paled. His wife grunted at him. "Stop your complaining, Marvin. It wasn't the little Amish girl's fault. You had to stand there right in the way of Miss Silicone USA and play with your phallic symbol—"

"Why don't you both help yourself to wine and a snack in the parlor," Sarah suggested with a brittle smile, trying desperately to resurrect her hostess image.

The Mortons went off in the direction of the

front parlor, grumbling at each other. Sarah heaved a sigh, wiping the back of her hand across her brow. She slumped against the kitchen counter and looked up at Matt with a woebegone look to rival the basset hound's.

"Well," he said with a grin. "That was exciting."

"It was terrible."

"Yeah," Matt agreed. "But it was funny."

Sarah's lips twitched and she gave in to the laughter. It had been a disaster. The first time Ingrid had left her in charge of the inn and within five minutes of the guests' arrival they were getting knocked senseless and threatening to sue. Still she couldn't help but see the funny side of it, and it felt good to laugh with Matt. It probably felt too good, but she didn't want to think about that now; she just wanted to share this moment with him. She watched the humor wipe away the lines of weariness in his handsome face and light up his dark eyes, and her heart gave a great big thump in her chest.

Matt watched her laugh, her clean, pretty face taking on a rosy glow, and his heart gave an answering thump. He reached out for her hand, just needing to touch her, and when her fingers curled around his, warmth spread through him like sunshine.

"Want to go share some wine and cheese with Marv and Peg?" he asked softly.

"Not really, but I suppose we'd better."

They walked out of the kitchen together like pals, Matt with an arm draped across Sarah's slim, square shoulders, smiles lingering on their mouths.

"Can I ask you a question?" Sarah said.

"Anything."

"What's a phallic symbol?"

"Ah . . . um . . ." He cleared his throat and dodged her questioning gaze. "I'll tell you later."

"Maybe you can show me?" she asked innocently.

Matt groaned, rolling his eyes heavenward. "I sincerely hope so."

Things just got curiouser and curiouser as the evening went on. It was the practice at Thornewood for guests and hosts to gather in the parlor to chat after dinner. Breakfast was the only meal served at the inn, so guests trekked into Jesse for their evening meal. Upon returning they were offered coffee or cocoa or brandy and fresh baked cookies as well as conversation.

This was something Ingrid and John pulled off with great success, both of them having excellent educations and a wide range of travel experiences. Sarah, however, had been outside the county only once, to visit relatives in Ohio, and her formal education had ended, as it did for all Amish children, at fourteen. Confronted with the role of hostess, she seemed to forget that she was quite well-read and had some understanding of current affairs gained through the pages of Ingrid's *Newsweek*.

Of course, it didn't help matters that the current guests were . . . well, strange.

Sarah sat in her chair unable to think of anything much to say while the Mortons and Lisbeth Parker stared at her as if she were an oddity in a museum.

Matt cleared his throat in an attempt to break the silence. "Mrs. Parker, it's too bad your husband wasn't feeling up to joining us."

She gave Matt a vacant look, then flinched as if she'd been pinched, and batted her long false lashes at him. "Oh, well, travel doesn't agree with Tim," she said, pouring a little brandy into her coffee. "He has a delicate constitution."

"I'd be happy to take a look at him—"

"No! No," she repeated, calming herself. She resurrected her beauty queen smile and bestowed it upon everyone in the room. "It's nothing serious, I assure you. He simply needs his rest."

Matt's brows rose and fell as he looked across the room at Sarah. She gave a small shrug. As yet no one had seen the mysterious Tim Parker.

"I can imagine he needs lots of rest," Marvin

Morton growled, his eyes fixed on Mrs. Parker's fantastic bosom. His wife gave him a sharp jab in the ribs.

Mrs. Parker changed the subject abruptly, going into a long, bizarre account of her recent trip to her optometrist, who had prescribed a single contact lens that she could wear in either eye. No one seemed to know any appropriate comment to make about that—except Mr. Morton, who told her the guy was probably a shyster, as were most doctors. Matt ground his teeth for a minute, then launched onto a detailed explanation of the pro bono work he did at a free clinic in North Minneapolis. The point was lost on Marvin, who turned the discussion into a racist commentary on the abuses of the welfare system.

Sarah watched it all unfolding with a sense of dread and helplessness. She tried to imagine how Ingrid would have handled the situation, but could only think that Ingrid and John would never have gotten into this kind of conversational snake pit in the first place. Heavens, her whole adventure of running the inn was turning into a nightmare. She should have known better than to believe she could handle this. She was after all, despite her longings to the contrary, just a simple Amish woman. Dreaming about being a part of that other world and pulling it off were two very different things.

She looked around the room and bit back a moan of despair. Matt was plainly furious with Mr. Morton, who had expanded his monologue into anti-Semitism. Mrs. Parker was pouring another dollop of brandy into her coffee cup. Blossom was sneaking off with one of the beauty queen's heels. Some grand evening this was turning out to be. The evening from hell.

"So, you're Amish, Sarah," Mrs. Morton said, dragging the topic back to the one thing Sarah wanted most to avoid talking about. She was quite certain the imperfections in her hostess skills were already glaringly apparent to the one person she wanted most to impress—Matt. Now she would have the spotlight thrown on her background and way of life, which couldn't have been more separate from his if she had been from Mars. And he would be able to see how truly unsuitable for him she was.

And what was the difference? she asked herself. The sooner he came to his senses, the better for both of them.

"Yes, Mrs. Morton, I'm Amish," she answered politely.

"So what's that like?"

What an enormous question. Sarah sat with her hands folded in her lap, struggling to formulate a reasonable answer, but Mr. Morton beat her to it.

"You've seen what it's like, Peg. It's like living in a hippie cult commune."

"Mr. Morton!" Matt protested, all his new-found protective instincts rearing up inside him. He'd sat through the man's diatribe on every other minority group, but this was the end. This ingrate had insulted Sarah, Sarah the sweet and innocent, and Matt wasn't going to have her subjected to abuse of any kind.

"Well, it is," Morton pressed on, waving his cigar. "I read all about it. They mate up their young folks like sheep and most of them have two or three wives."

"Mr. Morton, that's enough!" Matt bolted out of his chair, ignoring the pain it caused him. He was too angry to notice something as trivial as cracked ribs. He leaned toward the older man with a menacing expression. "If you want to be a bigot at least have the decency to do it in the privacy of your own home."

"Bigot!" Morton exploded. He rocked himself up off the couch. "You can't call me that!"

"I just did."

"Matt, stop it!" Sarah jumped up out of her chair and tried to pull Matt back to his. He paid no attention to her efforts. He and the guest were nearly toe-to-toe, Matt towering over Morton like an angry avenging angel.

"You're a rude, ignorant bigot. And if you think for one minute that I'm going to sit here and let you insult Sarah and treat her like some sideshow tourist attraction, you had better think again. Furthermore, I think you owe Miss Troyer an apology."

Morton's whole fat head turned the color of a radish.

"Matt, stop it!" Sarah hissed behind him. She hooked a finger through a belt loop on his jeans and tried to tug him backward. He wouldn't budge.

"I'm not apologizing to anybody," Morton said with a snort.

"Then I think you'd better leave."

"Matt!" Sarah wailed. This was all she needed. As if her reign as manager of Thornewood hadn't gotten off to a bad enough start, Matt was going to go and throw out the guests!

"W-el-l," Mrs. Parker said, drawing the word into three syllables. Her gaze had turned glassy. She seemed to be able to focus only the eye with the contact lens in it, and that one she fixed on Morton. "I'm with Dr. Thorne. I think you're insuffer-ufferably rude," she said with a hiccup.

Morton snorted, "That doesn't mean much coming from a woman whose bra size is bigger than her IQ."

"I don't have to put up with that!" Mrs. Parker said with a gasp. She reached into her purse and pulled out a pearl-handled derringer and waved it around. She rose to her feet, wobbling on one heel, trying to aim the gun. "You big lump o' Yankee lard!"

Mrs. Morton screamed. Mr. Morton's cigar fell out of his mouth and set the couch on fire. Matt dove for Mrs. Parker and knocked the gun out of her hands. It went off with a loud pop, shattering a decanter of red wine, which spewed all over Mrs. Morton, causing her to believe she'd been shot and making her scream louder. Just to put the icing on the cake, Blossom rushed in howling at the top of her lungs.

The farce had reached its climax.

"I can't believe this," Sarah muttered. She stood, dazed, on the porch watching the taillights of the Mortons' car bob off into the dark distance.

"Good riddance," Matt grumbled.

Sarah turned on him. "I can't believe you did this!"

"Me!" he exclaimed, splaying a hand across his chest as if she'd just stabbed him. He was the picture of confused, thickheaded male innocence. "What did *I* do?"

"What did *you* do?" Sarah rolled her eyes and clamped her hands to the top of her head as if she were afraid her temper would force her hair to stand straight on end. "You had to start a fight with a guest!"

"Sarah, the man was insulting you!"

"Ridicule is nothing new to me. I would have handled it."

"Well, I handled it for you."

"I wouldn't have fought with him. It's not our way."

"Yeah, well, it's my way," Matt said in a huff of injured male pride. He jammed his hands on his hips and scowled. "If the Silicone Queen hadn't pulled that gun, I probably would have punched him in the nose."

"Wonderful. Violence to defend the nonviolent." Sarah shook her head at the irony. "I don't need a protector, Matt Thorne. I can take care of myself. I know you come from a violent world, but I am not a part of that world."

There it was, plainly spoken, the line between them drawn as clearly as if she had taken a stick and pulled it across wet sand. Matt leaned against the porch railing and knocked his head against a post. She was right. In his attempt to defend her innocence he had sullied it with violence. He had dragged her down to a low level by starting a fight over her. He sighed and closed his eyes. Had the world he lived and worked in so tainted him that he had become a part of the problem? He had only wanted to help, both in going to work at County General and in coming to Sarah's defense.

"I only wanted to help," he mumbled miserably.

Sarah was too caught up in her own worries to notice Matt's pain. A part of her thrilled to the idea of Matt rushing to her rescue like a knight on a white horse, but having that particular fantasy come true was undoubtedly going to cost her dearly. She could see it now. Ingrid would fire her and she would have no choice but to go back to the farm. Her father would try to take control of her life again, and she would end up miserable and married to Micah Hochstetler, doomed to a life of drudgery, never to have an adventure again.

"I'm going to lose my job," she said with a morose sigh.

Matt turned toward her, leaning his hips against the porch railing. "You won't lose your job. This was all my fault. I'll explain it to Ingrid." It was his turn to sigh as he thought of how his sister would receive the news. "I'll explain it to Ingrid and then she'll kill me with her bare hands. Will you come to my funeral?"

Sarah's mouth twisted into her crooked little wry smile. "Sure. I wouldn't miss it."

"Will you dance on my grave?"

"I don't know how to dance."

Reaching out, he pulled her into a loose embrace and swayed a little from side to side as he hummed a few bars of a tune. In the dim yellow light of the porch, his gaze caught Sarah's and held it, and the atmosphere of teasing and camaraderie altered into something thicker and softer and much more serious.

"I'll teach you to dance, Sarah," he said.

She looked up at him, her heart in her throat. She was leaning against his chest, her hands pressed to the warm cushion of his sweater and the solid muscle beneath it. She could feel his heart beating. He was no dream, no figment of her overactive imagination. He was a man who had defended her honor. He had held her while she cried and then kissed away her tears. He was the embodiment of every romantic fantasy she'd ever allowed herself.

She was falling in love with him. No. She wasn't just falling, she was in love with him. It seemed completely impossible; they'd only just met. But she realized in her heart that she had known him for a long time, for forever. She'd just never really believed she'd meet him or touch him or be tempted by him outside the safety of her dreams.

He leaned down and brushed his lips across hers, and longing pierced her heart like a needle.

"We'd best go back inside," a voice whispered. It sounded like her own, but she felt strangely detached from it.

"Yeah," Matt agreed, though he made no move to let her go. "I need to make sure the couch isn't still smoldering."

"I should check on Mrs. Parker."

Sarah started to move out of his arms. Matt straightened away from the railing. Their gaze never broke.

I love her, he thought with a jolt. The revelation came as an epiphany, glowing with a wondrous light. It stunned him. That was the "something different" he'd felt along with wanting her. Matt Thorne, Romeo of County General, man of the world, avowed bachelor and slave to his career, was in love for the very first time. He'd taken one look at little Sarah Troyer and fallen like a rock. He looked down at her now with a feeling of awe that couldn't have been exceeded had she suddenly turned to gold.

I love her.

He felt a rush inside him as if a fresh wind were blowing all the dirt out of the corners of his soul. Then he crushed her to him, his arms banding her to his body, his mouth taking possession of hers. He kissed her with a rapacious hunger, eager to taste her sweetness and claim it as his.

Sarah arched against him, responding to his kiss out of pure instinct and need. Her body sought the heat of his, softness pressing into masculine strength. Everything about the kiss overwhelmed her and saturated her, and she wondered dimly if this was what it was like to be drunk. Drunk on passion. Drunk on desire.

She gulped it in with a spirit that had been thirsty all its life. She welcomed the thrust of his tongue, the feel of his tender, sensitive hands pressing down her back and over her hips, lifting her into the curve of his arousal.

"Sarah, I want you," he whispered, peppering her face with quick, ardent kisses. "I want you so much."

Want. What she knew of the word could have filled a book. She had wanted so much for so long, wanted so many things she wasn't supposed to have, wasn't supposed to need. She wanted Matt Thorne, in her bed, in her life, in her heart. He said he wanted her, but his life wasn't here. It was a world away, a world that would run roughshod over a naive Amish woman. Not that he would take her to it. Matt was by nature a charmer, a womanizer. He might want her now, but in a week or a month he would leave and she would be the one left wanting.

"I have to go inside," she whispered, and like the coward she was, she turned and fled to the relative safety of a house where the only other person was a drunken aging beauty queen who wore only one contact lens, carried a gun in her purse, and was married to an invisible man.

Matt watched her go, too undone by the explosion of emotion he'd experienced to go after her. He'd just discovered he was in love for the first time, and the object of that grand emotion was running away from him. Another first: He had no idea what to do about her. He had wooed and won nurses and neurosurgeons and even a CPA who had an MBA from Harvard—no mean feat—but he had no idea how to go about winning a sweet, gentle Amish girl. She wasn't impressed by his possessions or his clothes or his profession. None of the usual props would do. And maybe that was only right. Real love, the kind he was feeling, wouldn't go in disguise.

Blossom clambered up the porch steps, her long body wiggling like a centipede's. She plopped herself down on Matt's feet, looked up at him, and let out a long, mournful howl.

"Yeah," he muttered, wincing against the noise. "Sing one for me while you're at it."

7

The inn was silent. Mrs. Parker had surrendered her pistol for safekeeping in a locked cabinet and had retired, presumably to relate the evening's events to the enigmatic Tim, who hadn't been roused from their room even by the sound of gunfire. Ingrid's lovely hunter-green camelback sofa sat under a thick layer of fire extinguisher foam like a small volcano that had been rendered dormant. The parlor windows had been opened to fumigate the room with fresh night air.

Sarah moved around her small room with no energy, but no desire to go to bed either. She wasn't going to sleep. She would only lie there, tossing and turning, yearning for a man she couldn't have.

For a while she just sat on the bed looking at the room around her. The walls were a buttery shade of gold, decorated with a hand-painted ivy vine that trailed along the baseboard and around the lace-draped window. Aside from that, there were no adornments of any kind. In keeping with Amish ways there were no pictures or wall hangings. The curtain was fancier than anything in her mother's house.

Ordinarily, Sarah thought of this austerity as a simple rule to be followed. Tonight the plainness left an aching emptiness in her. It seemed symbolic of her life, devoid of tangible, touchable happiness. She knew she was supposed to find her happiness in her faith, and she had tried and prayed, but there was simply something missing, and no matter how hard she tried, she couldn't make that feeling go away.

She wondered as she undressed if she would have felt this way had Samuel lived, had their son lived. There was no way of knowing. In all honesty, Samuel had never been able to extinguish the longing in her. Maybe children would have filled that void, but there had been only one, and that child, Peter, had died of pneumonia before he had seen his first birthday.

She hung her plain blue dress in the closet beside her two other plain blue dresses, pulled on a simple white cotton nightgown, and went to the dresser to brush her hair. Sitting on the oak bureau was the little vial of *Evening in Paris* perfume and her *Glamour* magazine. Feeling defiant, she took the top off the perfume bottle and dabbed some of the oily liquid at the base of her throat. The smell was strangely sweet and foreign to her, but she decided she liked it, simply because it was something she wasn't supposed to have.

She flipped through a few pages of the magazine, her sense of rebellion building in her like a ball of compressed energy. Her eyes wandered over ads and articles, and she felt somehow less of a woman for never having worn panty hose or makeup. What possible sin could there be in wearing panty hose? How could a pair of aerobic shoes—whatever they were—corrupt her soul? Of course, she knew the standard answers to those questions—*Be ye not of the world and worldly things*—but it all seemed so petty to her. The way she saw it, the real issues of life had nothing to do with wearing lipstick or driving a car.

Frustrated, she heaved a sigh and left the magazine open on the dresser. She grabbed her robe and a towel and headed for the bathroom.

Matt lay on his bed, staring up at the ceiling. He was still dressed. The mind-numbing weariness that had plagued him since the attack was nowhere to be found tonight. All he could think about as he looked up at the dancing shadows of branches on the ceiling was Sarah. She hadn't spoken a response when he'd told her he wanted her, but there had been a mixed message in her wide eyes. Desire and fear. She wanted him too. He knew that in the way a man in tune with women always knew, by her kiss, by the change in her breathing, by the subtle scent of her skin. But she was afraid of that wanting.

Well, surprise, Sarah Troyer, because I'm afraid of it too. This new love was an unknown thing to him. He didn't know what to expect of it. Certainly, he had always cared for the women he made love with, and he had always been a considerate partner in bed, but the rules had changed now. The game was different. The stakes were higher. He wanted to give something he'd never given before—his heart. That was scary.

But he was getting ahead of himself, he thought, pushing himself carefully upright. Before he could give Sarah his heart, he had to make sure she would stick around long enough to take it. He had come up with a couple of ideas on the subject of courtship. Tomorrow he would begin the campaign.

He shed his sweater and undid the button on his jeans, then limped barefoot toward the bathroom door, intending to get a glass of fresh water to wash down his nightly dose of pills. His hand stilled on the knob, and he listened intently for a moment. He had heard the tub running earlier and had tortured himself for awhile with the mental image of Sarah bathing, but that had been an hour ago. He heard nothing now and he tried to squelch his disappointment as he turned the knob and swung open the door.

Sarah stood beside the tub, her hair up in a haphazard topknot with streamers of chestnut silk floating loose around the edges. She wore noting but a soft blue bath towel and a look of wide-eyed surprise.

Matt held his breath lest this vision disappear. He knew he should have done the gentlemanly thing and backed out, closing the door and leaving Sarah to her privacy. He knew that was what he should have done, but there was no way in hell he was going to do it unless she told him to.

Desire sprang to life inside him, a sleeping beast awakened, coiling fire in his gut. The air in the bathroom was warm and steamy, pungent with the scent of heated perfume and woman. And Sarah stood there clutching her towel above her breasts, beads of water still clinging to her smooth bare shoulders. She looked up at him, her eyes midnight blue, her lips damp and slightly parted.

The tension built and tightened around them like an invisible web. Matt let go of the door and took a step closer. Sarah watched him without moving, without speaking, without breathing. He looked completely male and predatory. His black hair was mussed, strands falling across his broad forehead. His dark, glittering gaze was narrow and intense. His face was taut, all the planes and angles emphasized. His jaw had already begun to darken with a beard. The strong, clean lines of his chest had taken on a sheen from the steam or from perspiration, she didn't know which. Her gaze trailed down past the white tape around his ribs to the undone button at the waist of the jeans that were clinging to his lean hips, and lower, to the evidence of a strong and immediate desire.

Everything basically female in her stirred and throbbed. She was suddenly conscious of the weight of her breasts and the sensitive flesh knotting at their tips. And low in her belly a tight fist of need tormented her.

"I want you, Sarah," he whispered.

Want. That word had haunted her all of her life. She wanted something to fill the gap in her heart. She wanted Matt Thorne. She wanted him now and she would want him still when he had gone. Why couldn't she, just this once, give in to the wanting? She wanted so badly to know what it was to have a man touch her with the same longing that was in her soul. She knew it wouldn't last. She knew that he would go and she would be left to her quiet life of duty. Couldn't she at least be allowed a beautiful memory to sustain her through a lifetime of longing and lonely nights? Who would that hurt? Where was the sin in wanting to be loved?

Her fist tightened briefly, then relaxed, and
the towel fell away.

Matt drank in the sight of her, thinking that
this was what a woman was supposed to look
like—soft and curvy, her skin glowing, her
breasts full, hips rounded. He ached to touch
her, to mold those ripe curves to the angular
hardness of his own body. Closing the distance
between them, he felt the web of sensuality
wind tighter around them. He breathed in the
scent of it, tasted it on his tongue, then he
leaned down and tasted Sarah, pressing his
mouth to the spot where neck met shoulder.
His hands skimmed up her sides to claim her
breasts, testing the weight of them, brushing
his thumbs across the distended peaks of her
dusky peach-colored nipples. He caught her
gasp in his mouth, rubbing his lips over hers.

Sarah melted against him. She felt hot and
boneless and alive in a way she never had before. She pressed herself against Matt, moaning deep in her throat at the exquisite abrasion
of his chest hair against her nipples. His hands
slid down her back, tracing lightly over the
hollows and ridges, sweeping down to cup
her buttocks. His fingers kneaded her flesh,
stroked, caressed. All the while his kiss sent
her mind spinning, cartwheeling beyond all
sense and control. Only two thoughts held fast:
She loved him and she wanted him. Beyond
those two thoughts was only sensation.

He bent her back, his body curving over hers like an archer's bow, strong and taut. His arousal nudged her belly, urging her to press her hips tighter to his. He trailed his mouth down the column of her throat, his tongue flicking out to catch the beads of moisture left over from her bath. The scent of cheap perfume burned his nostrils, and he smiled at the idea that Sarah, so devoutly plain and simple, was still a woman at heart and pampered herself with hour-long baths and dime-store cologne. He let himself think she had put it on especially for him, and the idea sharpened the edge of his desire even more.

He brought his mouth back up her throat, to her ear, to her temple. He raised his hands to undo the knot in her hair, then stood back a fraction of an inch so he could watch the shining waves tumble down. She was beautiful and she was his, and Matt had never wanted so badly to sweep a woman up into his arms and carry her to his bed as he did in that moment. He moved to do just that, then checked himself, reminding himself it wasn't the prudent thing to do, considering his injuries.

Sarah stared up at him, her eyes dark with passion, her mouth swollen from his kiss. She moistened her lower lip with the tip of her tongue as she moved a hand to touch the quivering muscles of his belly, and a hot surge of adrenaline scorched away what little sense he had left.

He led her across the room and placed her on his bed. She pulled the sheet up over her breasts as she watched him hook his thumbs inside the waistband of his jeans. Denims and briefs descended together and he stepped out of them and came to the bed naked except for his bandages. Naked, beautifully aroused, overwhelmingly male.

"Are you nervous, sweetheart?" he whispered, gently tugging the knot of sheet out of her fist and drawing it away from her body.

Sarah glanced up at his face, trying to come up with a witty remark, but her brain refused to cooperate. It had been a long time for her and she had only ever been with one man, a man who had only ever been with one woman. She was suddenly filled with such an overwhelming sense of inadequacy, she was afraid she might actually start to cry. She wanted so badly to please Matt, but she wasn't at all sure she knew how to go about it. He was bound to have sophisticated tastes and know all the subtle secrets of making love, while she knew only that she loved him.

"I'm nervous too," Matt admitted quietly. The bed dipped beneath his weight as he stretched out beside her. He propped himself up on one elbow and looked down at her face in the thin silver light filtering through the window. "I want so much to please you, Sarah," he murmured, echoing her thoughts. Then he set himself to the task.

He captured her left breast in his free hand and rubbed his thumb gently over her nipple, drawing a soft gasp from her. Murmuring words of approval, he bent his head and caught the tender bead in his mouth, sucking, caressing it with his tongue. Sarah's back arched off the bed. She tangled her hands in his short dark hair and moved restlessly beneath him. Electric sensations swirled beneath his mouth and shot all through her, congregating in the pit of her belly.

Knowing exactly what she was feeling, Matt slowly slid his hand down, over the soft slight swell of her tummy and lower, pressing gently with the heel of his hand, groaning in satisfaction as she lifted her hips into the pressure. He cupped her feminine mound, his fingers massaging her soft, warm flesh, parting the delicate petals to stroke the heart of her desire.

Sarah stiffened and moaned, swamped by sensation and yet wanting more. She ran her hands over Matt's strong shoulders, learning every muscle that lay beneath the smooth warmth of his skin. As he slid up her body she let her fingers explore farther still, down the solid columns of flesh that flanked his spine, down to the rounded firmness of his buttocks.

As he bent to kiss her again he caught her by

one wrist and pulled her hand over his hip to wrap it firmly around his erection, showing her exactly the way he liked to be stroked. His whole body shuddered at the pleasure of having her touch him, claim him. Her small fingers explored the length of him, wrung gasps from him as she feathered touches across his velvety tip, stroked downward to cup him. Matt returned the pleasure, sliding his fingers once more through the tight nest of curls at the juncture of her thighs to tease and to test her readiness.

"I want so much to please you," he whispered again as he shifted his weight and knelt between her legs. "Sarah. My sweet, sweet Sarah."

As he painted kisses across her face he pulled a pillow down from the head of the bed and eased it beneath her hips. Then, with tender care and touching hesitancy, he eased himself inside her. Slowly, savoring every inch she allowed him, sucking in his breath at how tight and hot she was. He paused to stroke her and groaned aloud when she tilted her hips up and took the whole length of him. There was mind-numbing sexual pleasure, but there was pleasure of another kind as well. A bright, wonderful sense of joy filled his chest as he sank down into Sarah's arms. This was the woman he loved.

He brushed two crystal teardrops from the

web of her lashes with his thumbs. "Sarah?" he whispered, his heart hammering in his chest. "Are you all right? Did I hurt you?"

The smile that stretched across her face doused his fear. Beneath him she rolled her hips in a way that made the air tighten like fists in his lungs. He let his body answer hers with a deep reaching stroke.

Sarah sighed his name in her mind, in her heart. She may have even spoken it aloud, but she was beyond knowing or caring. All she could think of was the perfect sense of rightness and of completion she felt joining with him. This was the man she had been waiting for all her life, the missing piece of her soul. This was the man she loved.

She wrapped her arms around him and moved with him, letting her spirit fly higher and higher, embracing the feeling of freedom that had suddenly been let loose inside her. She arched against him, taking him deep and urging him deeper still. He moved within her strongly, rhythmically. He kissed her mouth, her neck, his breathing echoing hers in gasps and pants that came faster and faster. He traced his tongue over the shell of her ear, whispered a word she didn't understand, a plea, a command. She raked her fingers down his back and pulled him hard against her as she arched upward into his thrust, and the night seemed to explode around them and in-

side them in starbursts of color and waves of
love.

The faint sound of the wind rattling the
dried leaves of the tree outside the bedroom
window was the first sound that penetrated
Sarah's numbed consciousness. She blinked
and listened, lying very still. Amazing. The
world still existed. It seemed unchanged. How
could that be? *She* had just changed radically.
She felt as if every cell in her body had been
rearranged and then infused with a powerful
elixir that made her feel at once euphoric and
energized and languid.

She waited for some sense of guilt or shame,
but neither assaulted her. Matt was not her
husband. She had known him only a matter of
days. Yet she had lain with him, shared her
body with him. She had been raised to believe
such behavior was sinful, but she didn't believe
it now as she lay in the warm circle of Matt's
arms. She loved Matt Thorne. In the world
they were poles apart, but in her heart they
were soul mates. No matter what came of it,
no matter what happened she would not regret
that she had given herself to him in the name
of that love.

Matt shifted beside her, taking more of his
weight off her and lifting himself up on one elbow. He grimaced as she stretched to switch

on the bedside lamp, then settled once again beside her.

"Well," he said. "You keep telling me I ought to be in bed. Are you happy?"

Happy? Happy didn't begin to cover it. But she was unaccustomed to talking with a man after making love—Samuel had found sex a duty and talk afterward unnecessary—and she wasn't sure what kind of response was appropriate at any rate. It struck her as unseemly to give him a critique of his performance, and she wasn't sure she wanted to hear one. She ducked her head and dodged his eyes, fumbling for the edge of the sheet.

Matt was touched by her shyness. He knew without asking, Sarah didn't just jump into bed with every halfway decent guy who came down the pike. She radiated innocence and inexperience, both of which excited him, and he wondered vaguely if that made him some kind of pervert. He'd just made love to an angel and, instead of feeling guilt about it, he felt powerful and male, vulnerable and in love. The strange mix of feelings swam inside him as he stared down at her.

"I'm happy," he whispered. He traced the back of a finger along her far cheek, turning her face gently and leaning down to kiss her. Lifting his lips just a heartbeat from hers, he looked into her eyes and said, "I can't remember the last time I was this happy."

It was the truth. For a long time now he had felt nothing but weariness and cynicism. He had maintained a frantic pace to his life more to distract himself from falling into despair than anything else. He had set out to achieve a goal that was unobtainable, and the disappointment had taken much of the joy out of his life. But that life was a long way away just now. Here, in the country, he felt cleansed and at peace. Here, lying next to Sarah, he felt happy and whole.

"Me too," she murmured, sharing his sense of completion.

"I know it seems like this is all happening too fast," Matt said, giving voice to the obvious argument. "I know it's only been a few days. But I know what's in my heart, Sarah. I'm falling in love with you."

Sarah stared up at him, her eyes as wide and dark as a new moon. Falling in love. She had finally realized where the saying had come from. Every time she looked at Matt she felt half-dizzy. It was the same sensation she got when she dreamed she was falling from some towering height. Now he was telling her he felt it too. She was too stunned to say anything.

"I've never said that to a woman before," Matt confessed.

"Why not?"

"Because it wouldn't have been the truth. No woman has ever gotten as close to me as you have. I guess I haven't allowed it. I've always put my career first. It doesn't leave much time for anything else."

She wanted to ask what now, but she bit her tongue and held the words back. Matt had finally had a few extra minutes in his schedule to fall in love, but his career was still there waiting for him in the Cities. She didn't want to hear him say what she knew was the truth, that he would go back to his job, that this time he was allowing them now would dry up and disappear and the love would be just a fading memory.

"I love you too," she whispered, smiling when he smiled. She couldn't let future sadness intrude on what she was feeling now. And it didn't matter that it was crazy to love him so soon or at all, that there was no future in it. She was in love with him right now, and it felt wonderful.

He traced a finger along her chest just above the edge of the sheet, the hooked the crisp cotton fabric and drew it slowly down, his eyes on Sarah's the whole while. A bloom of color blushed high across the apples of her cheeks.

"You don't have to be shy with me, sweetheart. I'm a doctor. I've seen lots of naked bodies."

Sarah's straight brows pulled together low over her eyes. "That is supposed to make me feel better?"

Matt chuckled at the unmistakable flare of jealousy in her eyes. "None of them were quite as sweet and pretty as yours."

She sniffed. "Ingrid warned me you were full of flattery."

"I'm surprised she didn't tell you I was full of something else."

"She did," she said, unable to keep her wry smile from curving her mouth. "But you don't smell like a cow yard so I guess she was exaggerating."

"Oh, very funny," Matt said sardonically, throwing a leg over hers and raising himself above her, a smile twitching at the corners of his lips. His dark eyes twinkled like starlight. "You'll pay for that remark, Sarah Troyer. I feel it only fair to warn you that doctors are trained to know the body's most ticklish spots."

"No! Oh, Matt! No!" She squealed and squirmed beneath the onslaught of his knowing fingers, twisting the sheets and rocking the bed as she struggled. "Matt! Don't! Stop!"

His fingers stilled at the sides of her breasts, and he stretched himself out on top of her, trying not to laugh too hard out of deference to his ribs. He rubbed his nose against the tip of Sarah's. "We'd better hold it down. Mrs.

Parker is liable to come charging in here and blow us away. We might even wake the elusive Tim."

Sarah giggled and shifted her hips beneath him, making their contact more intimate. Their gazes caught and heated. "You're not doing a very good job of keeping it down," she whispered in a husky voice.

"No, I'm not," he murmured, rocking gently against the heat of her.

Matt watched her intently as her eyes drifted shut and her face tightened in concentration. He dipped inside her and withdrew. She caught her breath and sighed.

He lowered his head and sampled the soft flesh at the side of her throat. Slowly he made his way down her body, lavishing attention on every inch of skin, nuzzling the full underside of her breasts, kissing the tiny mole just above her left hipbone, rubbing his nose across her belly button.

He pushed the sheet down farther, raising his head to study the downy nest of dark curls that cloaked her femininity when something else entirely caught his attention. Stretch marks. They were faint, but they were unmistakable to a trained eye. Matt traced a finger along the line that angled from her right hip.

"You had a baby," he whispered, feeling the

most alarming sense of disappointment that it hadn't been his.

Sarah met his gaze, wondering if the news would make her less desirable to him. "Yes," she whispered in return. "He died."

"Oh, Sarah." Matt slid up beside her once again and leaned over her, stroking her hair back, his dark eyes full of sympathy. The pain he felt for her was as strong as if the loss had been his too. "I'm sorry. What happened?"

"Pneumonia. We didn't realize until too late. The doctor said it was just the croup, but then it got worse so quickly. . . ."

"The doctor?" Matt said, tensing, anger rising up inside him. "Coswell?"

"Yes."

"That man isn't fit to take care of monkeys. He ought to be drummed out of the profession." He started to say something else, but Sarah lifted a hand and pressed her fingers to his lips.

"*Bitte*," she whispered, begging his understanding with her eyes. "It's in the past. Nothing can bring Peter back. Let's not talk of it now. I don't want to be sad tonight, only happy. Please, Matt. Only happiness. Only good things tonight."

"All I want is to make you happy," Matt said, pushing his anger aside for Sarah's sake. He leaned down and kissed her with such tenderness, it brought a lump to his throat. "I love you."

He trailed his lips along the delicate line of her jaw and let his hands set off on another fingertip tour of her body. She moved restlessly beneath him, her skin heating with the flush of desire.

"Matt?"

"Hmmm?"

"What you whispered in my ear before—what did that mean?"

He raised his head and looked at her, confused for a moment, then it dawned on him—both what he had whispered in the throes of passion and why Sarah hadn't understood what he meant. Of course she wouldn't have the same sexual vocabulary he had, if she had one at all. He smiled and leaned down again to nibble at her earlobe.

"You remember that incredible explosion that happened afterward?" he said in a voice warm and silky with passion remembered and renewed.

"Yes."

"That's what I wanted to have happen."

"Oh." She caught her breath again and moaned as he lifted her hips and entered her, filling her. It was an incredible sensation, being claimed by him, feeling not only her body but her soul invaded by him. Her mind fogged as he began to move, and she whispered breathlessly, "Do you want it to happen again?"

"Oh, yes, sweetheart," he answered on a heartfelt groan. "Oh, yes."

8

Matt woke alone. He wasn't particularly surprised, but he was disappointed. He wanted to lie beside Sarah and watch the soft light of dawn fall on her face. He wanted to watch her drift up out of sleep layer by layer until she blinked open those incredible blue eyes. The first thing she would see would be his face and she would smile and they would kiss and he would make love to her. Instead, he had nothing beside him but a rumpled pillow, no sweet lips to kiss, no soft body to ease the throbbing ache of his arousal; just the space where she had slept beside him and the faint scents of sex and perfume.

He rolled onto his back and cast a slit-eyed glance at the clock on the nightstand. Seventhirty. Sarah had probably been up for an hour, seeing to her chores. When he breathed deep, he could smell breakfast cooking.

He wondered how she would react to him today. She had certainly responded to him during the night. Lord, she had exhausted him. Making sweet, thorough love to her twice had drained his depleted energy reserves. He'd slept liked a dead man. He wondered now if she would be shy with him today or if she might be feeling regrets. He hoped not, because he sure as hell wasn't. He might not have felt certain about anything else in his life, but he was sure of one thing—he wasn't going to let Sarah slip away from him. She was his.

"Why don't you tell secrets to a pig?" Jacob asked. His eyes sparkled with mischief as he waited for his sister to answer his riddle. He took a big slurp of milk and set the glass back down on the table, nearly overturning it as he reached for a fresh hot muffin from the basket.

Sarah gave him an indulgent smile as she bent to take a coffee cake out of the oven. What she missed most about not living at home was seeing Jacob every day. She was well aware that in her heart he had taken the place of the son she had lost. The only harm she saw in that was that she was much too attached to him considering their current living arrangements. She looked at him now with his blond hair pressed flat from his hat and a big milk mustache framing his upper lip and felt a surge of warmth inside that had nothing to do with the heat of the oven.

"I don't know," she said, coming up behind him and pressing her oven mitts to his cheeks while he looked at her upside down. "Why don't you tell secrets to a pig?"

"Because pigs are squealers!" he announced and dissolved into triumphant giggles at having stumped his sister.

Sarah laughed with the sheer pleasure of watching Jacob, then went utterly still as the kitchen door swung back and Matt stepped into the room. After their night together, she was acutely aware of him as a male, even across a room. His gaze captured hers, and everything female in her came to attention. Her breathing grew shallow, her skin tingled. Having lain with him, touched him, felt him pressed against her and within her, she was much more aware of his body—the lean, muscled strength of it, the shape of it. The word handsome had taken on a stronger meaning for her. It was resonant in her mind as she looked at him now dressed casually in faded jeans that hugged his hips and thighs and a wine-colored jersey that emphasized his shoulders. For her, Matt Thorne was the living definition of handsome, and he was hers—at least for a little while.

The corners of his mouth turned up in a smile, and he went on looking at her as she went again to the stove, but when he spoke, it was to Jacob.

"What kind of wood is like a king?"

Jacob chewed his lip and screwed his face in

concentration, oblivious to the strong sexual currents humming between the adults in the room. Matt went on staring at Sarah, mouthing *I love you*. She blushed and glanced away, fussing with her oven mitt, unaccustomed to open declarations of affection. It wasn't the way of her folk to speak their feelings aloud, especially not in the company of others.

"Oak?" Jacob asked.

"Nope." Matt moved slowly across the room, skirting the big harvest table, stalking Sarah like a wolf stalking a deer. She glanced around nervously for an escape route.

"A pine tree?"

"Nope."

He corralled her up against the big institution-size stove. Sarah's heart was pounding frantically. Her gaze darted from Matt to Jacob, who was scratching his head as he stared at his muffin, still paying them no mind. Matt leaned forward to kiss her, and she turned abruptly so his lips just grazed her cheek.

Matt frowned, but moved away from her. He took the chair beside Jacob's and reached for a muffin. "Give up?"

The boy nodded.

Matt gave him a wink and a grin. "A ruler."

Jacob groaned and made a face, wriggling on his chair and hitting himself in the forehead with the heel of his hand, tipping his milk glass once again. Matt caught the tumbler and set it out of harm's way and tossed a napkin on the milk that had splashed onto the table.

"No school today again?"

"Today is Saturday," Jacob said, sneaking a piece of muffin under the table to Blossom. "Not even the English go to school on Saturday, Matt Thorne."

"How's the arm?"

"Much better. My mother put a milk poultice on it."

Pouring himself a cup of coffee, Matt nodded and made doctor noises. Sarah bent across the table to set down a platter of scrambled eggs, her face lowering to within inches of Matt's. He caught her eye and mouthed *I want you*. She gave a little gasp, her cheeks blooming, her eyes dodging to Jacob again.

Matt leaned back in his chair and studied her. This wasn't just shyness, this was something else, more like fear. She didn't want Jacob catching on to the fact that they were attracted to each other. That thought hurt. His feelings for her were tender and fragile. The idea that she was ashamed of what she felt for him was like poking a raw nerve with a needle.

"It still looks pretty terrible," Jacob said.

Matt dragged his attention away from Sarah

and back to her brother. "Still looks gross, huh?"

"I am not supposed to use that word. I got into trouble with it from my pop."

"You did? Gee, pal, I'm sorry. I didn't mean to get you in trouble."

"I know." Jacob nodded. He took a big bite out of his muffin and blueberry juice oozed down his chin.

"Still friends?" Matt asked, raising his brows.

The boy grinned, revealing a fresh gap in his smile where another baby tooth had disappeared. "Ya, sure."

"Great." He caught Sarah's gaze as she settled into the chair across from him and held it meaningfully for a moment. "What about you, Sarah? Are we still friends?"

"Of course," she answered just quickly enough to bring a guilty flush to her cheeks.

She wanted to go to him and hug him and rub a finger over the worry line that appeared between his eyebrows, but she couldn't with Jacob sitting there. All the boy would have to do would be to mention in passing that he had seen his sister kiss the English doctor, and a cloudburst of trouble would come raining down on their heads.

She gave Matt a look of apology, glanced at Jacob, then stared down at her empty plate.

The kitchen door swung back and Lisbeth

Parker sailed in wearing a lavishly fringed western blouse and a gallon of perfume. She wore her sunglasses again, undoubtedly hiding the aftereffects of the brandy she'd put away the night before. "Am I late for breakfast? I certainly hope I didn't keep y'all waitin'."

"No, Mrs. Parker." Sarah said, popping out of her chair like a jack-in-the-box, glad for a reason to dodge Matt's steady, condemning gaze. "We serve breakfast here until ten. If you'll have a seat in the dining room, I will bring you your meal."

"Oh, pooh." Lisbeth waved a dainty bejeweled hand. "I'll just sit right down here. I enjoy company while I eat."

"Mr. Parker won't be coming down?"

"No, no, I'm the early bird in the family. Tim is liable to sleep till noon. I wouldn't be surprised if we didn't see him at all today."

"Me neither," Matt mumbled into his coffee cup. Sarah smacked him with a hot pad as she moved around the table.

Mrs. Parker's gaze fastened on Jacob, and she made a little squeal of surprise. "Well, who have we here? Are you a little Amish boy? Well, aren't you just as cute as a bug!"

Jacob gave her a long look of open amazement, his gaze following the swinging fringe hanging from the precipice of her enormous bust upward to her sunglasses and her tower of auburn hair. "You have really big . . . hair."

Matt and Sarah released pent-up breaths as Jacob's final word came out.

"Jacob, manners," Sarah hissed between her teeth.

Luckily Mrs. Parker took his comment as a compliment and flashed her beauty queen smile all around. "Why thank you, honey. Aren't you sweet!"

"Did you sleep well, Mrs. Parker?" Matt asked, spreading butter on a hot muffin.

"Like a log. I declare, I wouldn't have heard a bomb go off!"

"Sarah will be glad to hear that, won't you, Sarah?" He glanced up at her as she settled in her chair once again, perversely enjoying the dark look she sent him. He was being childish, but he didn't care. "Mrs. Parker says she didn't hear a thing last night. How about Mr. Parker?"

"Slept like the dead."

"I spent half the night tossing and turning myself. How about you, Sarah?"

She picked up a carafe and thrust it at him. "More coffee, Dr. Thorne?"

"No, thanks. It keeps me up. It's just one of the things that can keep me up at night."

"You suffer from insomnia, Dr. Thorne?" Mrs. Parker asked as she trimmed the crusts from her toast and piled them beside her plate like tiny cord wood.

"Oh, I wouldn't call it insomnia, no. Would you, Sarah?"

Sarah sent him a fuming glare. "Jacob, why don't you and I go gather the eggs together?"

Jacob was halfway to the door as he answered. "I can't. I have to get home to help. We are stuffing the mattresses today. It's a big job."

Sarah felt a twinge of resentment as he disappeared out the back door, the pockets of his trousers bulging with muffins. It was followed closely by guilt. She had no right to demand Jacob's time; he was needed at home. Besides that, she should have been ashamed for wanting to use him for her own purposes. Both feelings, however, took a backseat to the need to get away from Matt. Mouthing words of love one minute and making suggestive remarks the next, he had her off balance again.

She pushed her chair back from the table. "Will you be needing anything else, Mrs. Parker?"

"No, no, honey. You go on with your little jobs," the woman said distractedly as she picked blueberries out of a muffin and made a smiley face with them on her place of scrambled eggs.

"Dr. Thorne will keep you company, then."

Sarah didn't even glance at Matt as she made her exit. She wanted to get out into the fresh air where she could think. In the com-

forting dark of night she hadn't given much
thought as to how she would deal with Matt
during the day. In the comforting dark of night
she could be anything she wanted to be. With
the rising of the sun came the sure fact that
she was nothing but an Amish woman. How
else was she supposed to behave? She knew
nothing of taking a lover; in truth, knew little
about physical intimacy. She had experienced
more in one night with Matt than she had in
all the time she'd been married to Samuel.

He seemed hurt that she hadn't been openly
affectionate with him in the kitchen, but that
kind of behavior was foreign to her. Even if
Jacob hadn't been there as a set of eyes and
ears for Isaac, Sarah didn't know if she could
have done it. Their loving was a very private,
very personal thing to her; she didn't want to
share it with anyone who happened to be looking their way. What passed between them
would be a secret because that was the way it
had to be and that was the way she wanted it.
When he left, she would keep that secret
locked in her heart, taking it out at special
times to appreciate like a treasure.

"Can I help?"

She looked up sharply, freezing in the motion of snatching an egg from beneath a doz-
ing red hen. Matt stood in the doorway,
blocking out much of the morning light. "No,"

she said, returning to her task. "Seems you can only hurt."

"Well, you would know all about that, wouldn't you, Sarah?" He made no move to enter the henhouse, but turned and leaned his back against the doorjamb and crossed his arms over his chest. Blossom settled herself on his feet and stared at the chickens. The chickens watched the basset hound, making low sounds in their throats.

Sarah moved from roost to roost, plucking the eggs out of the straw beds with a stealth and speed bred from long experience. She piled them carefully in a basket slung over her left forearm. She didn't know what to say to Matt. If she told him she was holding back because she didn't want other people to know about them, he would be hurt. If she told him she was holding something back because she knew in the end he would leave, he might just end it now, and she didn't want that. What she wanted was for the world to recede as it did every time he kissed her. What she wanted was to be transported to a different place and time where loving him wouldn't be difficult or dangerous or doomed to disappointment.

"Don't you regret it," he said tightly, turning to block her path as she neared the door. He dislodged the dog from his feet and planted himself squarely, filling the frame of the doorway like a gunslinger come to duel. "Don't you regret what we did last night, Sarah. It was beautiful and special. Don't you dare regret it."

"I don't regret making love with you," she whispered, staring down at her feet.

"What then? I spend the night making love with you, and in the morning you treat me like a leper. What conclusion am I supposed to draw from that?"

Sarah sighed, still not looking at him. What was she supposed to say? What was she supposed to feel? The answers to those questions were so much clearer when the adventure existed only within the safety of her imagination. The bliss of it was not clouded by issues then; there was no tomorrow to be wary of.

"I just don't know what you want from me," she murmured.

Matt watched her fight with her own inner questions, her straight brows pulling together above closed eyes, and a current of love and desire surged through him, making everything else unimportant.

"This," he said, coming forward and tilting her chin up. "This is what I want."

He settled his mouth over hers slowly and softly, cupping her face in his hands. The taste of him was heaven. The heat of his mouth and his body against hers seared away the cloud of doubt that had been hanging over her. Sarah responded to him without hesitation, letting him bend her back over his arm as he deepened the kiss. Arched against his solid body, she was oblivious to everything but the warmth that welled and glowed inside her. She wished with all her heart that they could just stay this way, but it wasn't to last. It wasn't to last more than a minute or so, because that was when all hell broke loose inside the chicken house.

Behind Sarah there was a growl and a chicken war cry, and suddenly it seemed as if a tornado had revved into high gear inside the close confines of the little shed. Chickens squawked as Blossom tore around in circles, baying her lungs out as she tried to nab a red hen. Two chickens hurled themselves against Sarah's back, wings beating frantically. She lunged forward in surprise, knocking Matt off balance. He went backward out the door, tripping and landing on his back in the dirt. Sarah stumbled after him, her skirts tangling around her knees. She sprawled forward and had to give up her hold on her egg basket to save herself. She ended up on her hands and knees. The eggs—at least some of them—ended up on Matt. The red hen shot out of the coop like a missile. Blossom, in hot pursuit, scampered under Sarah, then trampled across Matt's prone form.

"Wait'll they hear about this in the ER," an amused voice sounded from above him. "How

I caught the great Dr. Thorne with egg on his face."

Matt eased himself into a sitting position, wincing at the nip of pain in his ribs and the gooey mess on his chin. He wiped the egg away with his hand then stared in disgust at the yellow ooze on his palm, not sure what to do about it. He shot a glance at the woman who seemed so amused at his predicament, taking in battered dusty cowboy boots and legs that stretched a mile straight up. "Would you care to shut that lovely mouth long enough to give me a hand up, Nurse McCarver?"

She grimaced at the slimy palm he offered. "No way. The yoke's on you, Doc."

"You're a regular Florence Nightingale," Matt said sarcastically. "Has anybody told you your bedside manner stinks?"

"Not recently. You certainly never complained," she said sweetly, a wry smile canting her wide mouth.

Matt pushed himself to his feet, dusting off his jeans with his clean hand, then smearing the egg yolk onto his thigh, grumbling and scowling the whole time. He turned to help Sarah up, but she had already gotten to her feet and stood by the door of the chicken house fussing at brushing the dust from her apron, casting surreptitious looks at the woman who had come to call.

Julia McCarver stood grinning at them both,

her hands tucked into the back pockets of her tight faded jeans, her long mane of dark red hair tossing in the morning breeze. She had the lanky frame of an overgrown tomboy, a tomboy grown to just a hair's breadth under six feet, but she managed to exude femininity just the same. It emanated from her face, which was a study in delicate sculptured lines and exaggerated features. Her eyes were a rich chocolate-brown, enormous, limpid, sparkling, fringed by impossibly thick lashes; they gleamed with suppressed laughter and womanly secrets. Her mouth was too wide. Her lips were full and pouty, and they pulled back into a grin that was infectious.

She was beautiful and seemed friendly and obviously knew Matt—in the biblical sense, if Sarah had taken her comment about bedside manner right. She felt an instant burning rush of jealousy.

"Sarah, this is Julia McCarver," Matt said. "The nurse from hell. Julia, this is Sarah Troyer."

"Nice to meet you, Sarah," Julia said ebulliently. She offered Sarah her right hand while she snagged back a handful of hair with her left. "You have my condolences for having to put up with this grizzly bear while he licks his wounds."

She turned to face Matt, her look softening to genuine concern as she took his hands in hers and squeezed them. "All kidding aside," she said softly, "it's really great to see you on your feet again, you arrogant jerk." She leaned forward and gave him a small, chaste kiss on the lips.

Sarah thought she would choke on her jealousy. It rose in her throat like bile, and she couldn't even begin to force it back down. So much for Matt Thorne's profession of love. Well, she'd been warned, hadn't she? Ingrid had told her Matt was a ladies' man. What difference did it make anyway? She knew full well what they had together wasn't going to last.

"I'll leave you to your . . . visit," she said tightly. Snatching the egg basket, she strode for the house without looking back.

Julia raised one long curved brow and gave Matt an amused look. "So that's how the wind blows."

"Save the smart-ass comments, Julia," Matt warned. They had a long history of playful verbal warfare, but he was in no mood to be teased about Sarah. "Please," he added, softening the order to a request.

Julia studied him for a long moment, her wide, bright eyes searching. Finally she nodded. "Okay." She brushed a thumb across a smudge of egg yolk on his chin. "Why don't you go get washed up, then we can chat? I spied a swing on the front porch. I'll meet you there."

Matt went into the house, cleaned up and changed into fresh jeans and a burgundy chamois shirt. He had hoped to get a word with Sarah, but she was engrossed in a conversation with Lisbeth Parker and didn't do more than glance at him as he passed the parlor door.

Julia was waiting for him, sprawled comfortably on the porch swing. She had one booted foot on the bench, the other long leg stretched out, regulating the speed of the swing. It was hardly a feminine pose, but the usual rules didn't apply to Julia; she managed to look stunning regardless. And, as always, she seemed oblivious to her looks. She wore only a minimum of makeup. Beneath an oversize bomber jacket that had seen better days she wore an old white T-shirt with a faded "Life Run" logo on it. She gave him a crooked smile as he lowered himself to the bench.

"So, is all this peace and quiet driving you bonkers yet?"

"No," Matt answered truthfully. A part of him had expected it to; he was, after all, a city boy born and bred. He was used to the sights and sounds and smells and the tension in the air of a vibrant metropolitan area. He was used to the nerve-racking pace of the ER. The first couple of days he had been here the quiet

had irritated him, but at the moment he
couldn't say that he missed any of it.

Julia made no comment. She chewed her
lower lip and looked pensive, as if she took his
contentment as a bad sign. Matt glanced at her
and looked back out at the front yard. It was a
gorgeous Indian summer morning, unseason-
ably warm. The air was dotted with ladybugs
flying aimlessly around. The chains of the
porch swing squeaked.

"So how are you—really?"

"Better. As you can see, my face no longer
looks like an overripe melon. The ribs are healing. The leg . . . I don't know. Do you think
women would find a slight limp sexy?"

"They would if you were the one limping."

Matt reached over and tweaked her cheek.
He enjoyed the easy camaraderie that existed
between himself and Julia. They had been lov-
ers once, but it had been a disastrous affair
and in the end both had admitted to treasuring
their friendship too much to spoil it just for
the sake of fabulous sex.

"What about you?" he said. "How are you
doing?"

"Me?" she asked, feigning surprise. "Never
been better."

Matt wasn't fooled for an instant. "Have you
heard from him?" He didn't use a name because he couldn't bring himself to say it. He
hadn't liked quarterback "Storm" Dalton the

few times he had met him, and had never thought him good enough for Julia. It gave him no pleasure to know he'd been right all along.

"No," she said, picking at a scab of paint on the arm of the swing, giving her attention to the task as if it held some earth-shattering importance. "I don't expect to. He's playing for Kansas City now. He doesn't owe any loyalty to an old Vikings fan, does he?" She shot Matt a look. "Don't answer that. And don't say you told me so."

"I wasn't going to."

"Good," she said, forcing a smile. "Because I didn't come all the way down here to talk about me. I came to talk about you."

"What's up in the ER?"

"Same old stuff. The names and the faces change, but the score stays the same. We're outnumbered. We could use our top dog back. When are you going to be ready?"

Matt took a long time in answering. A lot of feelings surfaced at the thought of going back, some of them pleasant, most of them not. The truth was the top dog was feeling old and cynical and he couldn't even muster the enthusiasm to lie. "I don't know."

Julia pulled herself up, the seriousness of the topic demanding a more aggressive posture. "Matt, what happened—"

"This isn't about me getting shot, Julia. It's

about trying and caring too much and not being able to make a difference."

"You make a difference! I've lost count of
the lives you've saved."

"And I've lost count of the ones who came
back shot or knifed or OD'd or with a gun in
their hand so they could robe the drug cabinet."

"Those aren't the ones you're supposed to
count."

"Aren't they?"

"Come on, Matt, you thrive on the action.
It's only natural for you to feel a little de-
pressed now, but that will wear off. You just
need to get back in harness again. You need to
get back to the city, back to reality. Look
around you. This isn't reality. This is . . . is . . ."
She looked around as if an appropriate word
might pop out at her, finally shrugging. "This
is a cornfield."

Matt looked around. He saw the bleached
stalks of corn, heard them rustling in the
wind. He watched an Amish buggy pass. He
saw the sky as a bowl of electric blue, un-
marred by high-rise buildings. A dragonfly in-
vestigated the pot of yellow mums that sat on
the porch step, and Blossom sat like a sentinel
at the end of the driveway with a shoe in her
mouth.

Julia pushed the swing into motion again
with the toes of her boots, her hands dangling

between her knees, her gaze drifting to the far side of the yard where Sarah had come out to rake leaves. "So what's the story on you and Laura Ingalls Wilder?"

"I'm not ready to talk about it."

Julia gave a low whistle. "That serious, huh?"

Matt said nothing. He just gave her a long steady look with his dark eyes, letting her read what she would there.

Julia shook her head and heaved a sigh, her anger showing through her normally placid manner. "Will you look at what you're doing here?"

"I'm recuperating."

"You're hiding. You're retreating—not only from the city but from this century! Matt, you're too good a doctor to just burn out and fade away!"

He couldn't think of anything worth saying. Propping his elbows on his knees, he leaned forward and rubbed the back of his neck. Julia slumped back against the bench, spearing her fingers into her thick hair and smoothing it back from her face.

"Want to take a drive into town?" Matt asked. "They have a real old-fashioned soda fountain at the drugstore."

"No, thanks." Julia shook her head wearily and checked the man's watch she wore on her wrist. "I should head back. I told Devers I'd work her shift."

Matt pushed himself up from the swing and followed her to the porch steps, catching her by the sleeve of her bomber jacket when she was two steps below him. "You can't bury yourself in work forever."

She pressed her lips into a long thin line as she avoided his gaze. "I guess we all have our ways of compensating, don't we?"

Matt took the hint. He thought she was hiding; she thought he was hiding. He wasn't going to let her in on all of his feelings; she wasn't going to let him in on hers. Standoff. "I'll walk you to your car."

At the door of her Firebird she turned around and hugged him fiercely, then pulled back and swiped her hair out of her eyes. "Look, I know you're going through a rough spot right now. Just do me a favor and hang on, will you?"

He nodded, his gaze holding hers. "You too."

She managed a tired smile that didn't get anywhere near her eyes. "Yeah, sure."

Matt leaned against Lisbeth Parker's white Cadillac and watched Julia drive off, his mind resolutely shutting out the things she had said. As the Firebird disappeared down the road, he redirected his attention, catching Sarah looking at him.

Sarah dodged his gaze, focusing on her raking. She scraped the bamboo tines of the broad rake against the ground with more zeal than was required, sweeping the fallen maple leaves into an ankle-deep pile. It didn't matter to her that Matt had old girlfriends calling on him. Scrape, scrape, scrape. It didn't matter to her that Julia McCarver was beautiful. Scratch, scratch, scratch.

"Trying to rake your way to China?"

She stopped just short of raking over the sneakers that had come into her limited field of vision. "Any job worth doing is worth doing well."

She started to turn away from him, but he caught her by the shoulders. Still, she refused to look up at him. Tears had gathered behind her eyes and were pressing for release.

"Julia is an old friend of mine," Matt said softly. "There's nothing romantic between us. There hasn't been for a long time. She came to prod me about going back to work."

"It is no concern of mine," Sarah said primly.

"I'd like to think it is. Come on, Sarah," he said in his soft, cajoling tone. "Look at me. Please."

The please did her in. He sounded so sincere. She was being silly anyway, wasting what time they had together on pointless jealousy.

She gave him a weak version of her crooked smile.

"That's better," he said, tracing his thumb over the line of her mouth. A chuckle worked its way up out of his chest. "My little pacifist. You looked ready to tear Julia's hair out by the roots when she kissed me!"

"Make jokes," Sarah said, trying to look stern. "You bring out the dickens in me, Matt Thorne. You should be ashamed."

"Should I?" he asked softly. Suddenly the fresh fall air was charged with energy humming tight around them. Matt brought his hands up to frame her face, his thumbs brushing under the loose ties of her *kapp*. "I think I make you feel alive. I know that's how you make me feel. I think I bring that fire you keep buried inside you a little closer to the surface."

"Matt . . ." She breathed his name like a sigh, invoked it like a prayer. She tilted her chin up, offering her mouth to him, and her whole body jolted as he kissed her, as if he'd infused her with a sudden burst of electricity. Alive. That was exactly what he made her feel, beautifully, achingly alive.

When he lifted his head, he had that look of wonder in his eyes again and he smiled. "I never would have believed love could happen so fast," he murmured.

He slid his hands back from her face, tugging her *kapp* off and loosing the moorings of her bun all in one motion. Hairpins scattered, and her long chestnut tresses tumbled free, the wind catching at strands and fluttering them like ribbons. It felt wonderful and free—like her spirit.

She made a face at him. "Now, look what you've done. I'll have to put it all back up again. You're worse than a little boy tugging braids."

Matt laughed, unrepentant. He felt, if not like a little boy, certainly younger than he had in a long time. "Oh, yeah?" he said, rising to the bait. "In that case, I belt you can't get this away from me." He extended his arm above his head with Sarah's fine white *kapp* perched on the ends of his fingers.

Sarah made a jump for it. Matt snatched it back and twisted away from her. They played a laughing game of keep-away, eyes dancing, bodies dodging and feinting, leaves crunching beneath their feet. Matt was able to move at only about half speed. To compensate, Sarah didn't try as hard as she might have to win. The object wasn't in getting her *kapp* back, but in prolonging the game. They laughed and chased each other, touching and tickling. And as always, they became so absorbed in each other, the rest of the world faded into the far background. They scarcely noticed the sun that warmed them or the breeze or the dog that came to bark at their foolishness or the Amish farm wagon that rumbled past.

Matt tired first and gave up, sinking down into the pile of orange leaves, breathing heavily and grinning hugely. Sarah followed him without hesitation, her plain skirt billowing around her in a puddle of blue as she settled beside him. They sat facing each other, hip-to-hip. Sarah reached up and brushed at errant strands of black hair that had tumbled across Matt's forehead. He lifted a dried leaf and tickled the end of her nose with it. They both leaned toward each other simultaneously for a kiss, and Sarah thought her heart would burst with happiness. She was in love, and all was right with the world . . . at least for a little while.

9

"Thank you, Mrs. Parker," Sarah said, tucking the credit card slip into a desk drawer. "I hope you enjoyed your stay with us."

"It was just lovely, honey," Lisbeth Parker gushed. She tossed the end of her fox stole over her shoulder and glanced around for any sign of Blossom. "We had the nicest time, and you were just a doll! I sure wish we had some Amish people back home."

Matt rubbed his jaw, fighting the urge to say something nasty. Sarah just smiled her little Mona Lisa smile, unaffected by the comment. She knew people generally meant no harm when they said things like that, and taking remarks in stride was simply part of being Amish.

"You don't want to forget this," Matt said, holding out Mrs. Parker's pearl-handled pistol and ammunition.

"Oh, heavens no! I couldn't leave Li'l Abner!" She smiled at the gun as if it were a favorite pet and tucked it into the depths of her handbag. "Tim gave him to me our first Christmas together."

Matt stuck his hands in his trouser pockets and rocked back on his heels. "Isn't that sweet."

Lisbeth waved a hand and gave them a coy look. "He's like that, the big ol' darlin'. I'd best get on out to the car now before he loses his patience and starts in on that horn. It plays the Texas Aggie fight song. Drives me right out of my mind."

"Really?" Matt said, eyes alight. He winced as Sarah gave his arm a sharp pinch.

Lisbeth bid them farewell again as she turned and pranced out the front door, fox tails swinging. Matt rubbed his palms together and started after her. "Come on. We'll finally get to see if there really is a Tim."

Sarah grabbed his arm and held him back. "No! It's more fun not knowing."

Matt was incredulous. "Are you kidding? That woman and her invisible man have been driving me crazy all weekend!"

Laughing, Sarah tugged him into the parlor doorway so he wouldn't be tempted to peek out the window in the front door. She held onto his hand as she leaned back against the wide frame. "The mystery is more fun than the knowing would be."

"You think so?" Matt let the Parkers slip from his mind as he snuggled closer to Sarah, flanking her legs with his. He settled his hands on her waist, rubbing his thumbs lightly in a circular motion against her. "I don't know. You were a mystery to me, but getting to know you has been a hell of a lot more enjoyable than just wondering."

Sarah blushed prettily. They had spent a second night together in Matt's bed, but she still felt shy with him. "Such language," she teased. "My father would wash your mouth out with soap."

"Would he?" He slid his hands upward, just brushing the heavy underswell of her breasts. She closed her eyes and sucked in a breath. "What would he do to me for taking liberties with his daughter?"

She didn't answer. With her eyes still squeezed shut, she threw her arms around his neck, raised herself up on tiptoe and kissed him with a hunger that bordered on desperation. Matt didn't argue. He couldn't get enough of the taste of her or the feel of her against him. He wrapped his arms around her and returned her kiss, making love to her with his mouth.

"Let's go back to bed," he whispered, licking her earlobe.

"It's the middle of the afternoon," Sarah said, but it was more an observation than a protest. Her knees had gone weak at his suggestion.

"It's night somewhere," Matt muttered, planting kisses along her jaw, working his way back to her mouth. "I think it's night in England. We'll pretend we're in England."

"I've always wanted to go there," Sarah whispered, letting her mind clutch at dreams and desires, pushing reality aside.

There was a sudden bang in the front hall and a voice called out cheerily, "I'm ba-ack!"

Matt and Sarah bolted apart, Sarah ducking into the parlor to check her appearance in a mirror. Matt brushed the back of a hand across his mouth then stuffed his hands in the pockets of his trousers in an effort to hide the fact that he was half-turned-on. Another minute and he might have taken Sarah where they stood. Wouldn't that have been a nifty way to welcome his sister back.

Ingrid dropped her enormous suitcase at the foot of the stairs and gave him a shrewd look. "I see you're up and around."

Heat crept into his cheeks, but he managed to maintain a poker face. "Yes, I'm feeling much better. Good to see you home, sis." He bent and dutifully kissed the cheek she presented him. "Is everything all right up in Stillwater now? We weren't expecting you back for another day or two."

"Dorothy's husband was doing much better than they had first thought he would," she said, pushing up the sleeves of her oversize red sweater. She stuck a hand into the pocket of her snug black stirrup pants, dug out a note, checked it, nodded, folded it, and put it back all without breaking stride in the conversation. "They sent him home today. We didn't have any guests booked until Thursday, and Dorothy figured by then she would be more than ready to get back to work. So, here I am."

Ingrid heaved a sigh up into her fashionable tumble of black bangs and planted her hands on her slim hips. Three years older than Matt, she still thought of herself as Big Sister, despite the differences in their size. She was a tiny woman with a pixie's face and big dark eyes, but what she lacked in stature she made up for in energy and determination. Matt had long thought she had enough electricity in her to light up half of St. Paul.

She looked at him now with the critical eye of an art expert, her dark eyes taking in every aspect of his face, then moving down over his blue shirt and tan chinos, all the way to the tips of his sneakers and back up again. When she got back to his face she wore an expression of mingled anxiety and relief.

"It is so good to see you on your feet," she said, her voice suspiciously thick. "You don't know how afraid I was of losing you."

"Hey," he said, wrapping his arms around her and giving her a brotherly hug. "You can't get rid of me that easily."

"Hello, Ingrid. Welcome back," Sarah said, emerging from the parlor, cheeks still rosy with a blush, hands fussing with the folds of her black apron. She cast a quick, shy glance at Matt.

"Sarah." Ingrid disengaged from Matt's embrace and immediately hugged her friend and employee. "How did everything go? Let's go into the kitchen and have some tea and you two can tell me all about your adventures. Did anything exciting happen?"

She was already moving toward the kitchen with her brisk efficient stride, snatching up a stack of mail from the desk along the way.

"Just the usual," Matt said. "A little gunplay, a small fire. Nothing to brag about."

"Yeah, right," Ingrid said on a laugh as she shuffled through her mail and pushed the kitchen door open with her hip.

Sarah gave Matt a look. He just shrugged.

Over cookies and tea they told the tale of the Mortons and Lisbeth Parker. Matt offered to pay for the sofa as well as what Ingrid had lost when the Mortons had checked out, but she wouldn't hear of it. She said her insurance would cover the damage to the sofa and as for the Mortons, she could do without the money of people who insulted her friends.

Matt went on to relate all of Blossom's sins. Ingrid listened, smiling benignly, like a mother who was too blind to realize her much-adored child was a monster.

"And to top it off," Matt said, lifting an accusatory finger, "one of my favorite Loafers is missing. In fact, a number of shoes have disappeared."

"Really?" Ingrid said, the light of excitement in her eyes. "I wonder if she's making a nest somewhere. She's due to have puppies in a week or so."

Thunderstruck, Matt stared at his sister. "You mean you're going to have *more* of them?"

"Of course!" Ingrid leaned down and hefted the unwieldly dog onto her lap. Blossom settled herself, breaking into a big doggy grin Matt thought looked suspiciously smug. Ingrid rubbed the dog's ears and spoke to her in the childish way some adults used with babies. "We just *love* our Blossom, don't we?"

Blossom let out a little woof.

Matt rolled his eyes. "Jeez, Ingrid, get a life."

Ingrid ignored him, turning her attention to Sarah. "Sarah, I know it's not a church Sunday, but if you want to go visit your family, please feel free. I can handle the big guy here."

Matt scowled. Sarah sent him a little smile. She knew she should take Ingrid's suggestion and go to see her parents and siblings, but the truth was she didn't want to spend any time away from Matt. He was staying only for a

short while; her family would always be there.
"Actually, I thought I would just stick around
here today, but I should go out and see to my
chores."

She started for the back door and Matt rose
as well. "I'll go out with you."

"No, Matt," Ingrid said, her voice pleasant
enough, but there was a glint of steel in her
gaze that made him frown. "Stay with me. We
have a lot of catching up to do."

He settled back into his chair and watched
as Ingrid put Blossom down and casually went
to the window to look out at Sarah crossing
the yard.

"I had a chat with your local doctor—I use
the term loosely," he said. "I can't believe people actually line up to put their lives in his
hands."

"They don't have a choice," Ingrid said, returning to her chair. "The next nearest doctor
is thirty miles away."

"That's frightening."

"You don't know the half of it. Matt, good
doctors don't want to locate in rural areas like
this and you can well imagine why. The money
isn't great, the hours stink, there's no prestige,
no fancy country club to join, nothing to
aspire to."

"Who wants to be a general practitioner
when he can specialize and pull down twice
the bucks."

"You said it, not me. Consequently, towns like Jesse end up with doctors like Coswell."

"I wouldn't send Blossom to that guy."

"Neither would I. Thankfully, since this is prime farm country, our veterinarians are excellent."

Matt shook his head at the shame of it—a town where the people would have been better off being treated by the horse doctor. He nibbled thoughtfully on a chocolate chip cookie.

"I think you know what I want to talk to you about," Ingrid said quietly, her manner instantly changing the tone of the conversation. Her fingers toyed with a small envelope, turning it around and around in her hands, but her attention was solely on her brother.

Matt could feel her gaze on him, but he didn't look up. He loved his sister, but he didn't much care for being made to feel like he was twelve all over again. He put his cookie down and crossed his arms over his chest defensively. "What?"

"Sarah."

"What about her?"

"I'm not blind, Matt. She looks at you like you can walk on water."

He turned toward her then, his gaze calm and clear. "This is none of your business, Ingrid." His tone was soft and level, but the warning was unmistakable.

"Isn't it?" Ingrid put the envelope down and

leaned forward over the table. "Sarah is my friend as well as my employee. I care about what happens to her. I don't want to see her get hurt, Matt."

"What makes you think I intend to hurt her?"

"I don't think you *intend* to hurt her, but that's what's going to happen. I know you, Matt. Your head is easily turned. You've been cooped up in this house with only Sarah for company. She's a bright, sweet, pretty girl—"

"She's a woman, Ingrid, not some kid in pigtails," he interrupted, resenting the implication that he would take advantage of an innocent child, even though innocent was a word he had used himself to describe Sarah.

"Be that as it may," Ingrid said, not backing down in the least. "She's not the kind of woman you're used to. She's not someone you can just play with, Matt."

Matt gave a harsh, humorless laugh. "Boy, you certainly have a high opinion of me all of a sudden!"

Ingrid closed her eyes briefly, sighed, then tried again. "I'm not being critical. I know your career comes first with you and that's fine. The women you've been involved with know it too. I just don't think Sarah will understand those kinds of rules."

"Well maybe I'm not just playing with her. Has that thought occurred to you, Ingrid?" he

said in a voice low and rough with emotion.
He stared his sister in the eye and made what
was probably the biggest confession of his life.
"Maybe I'm in love with her."

Ingrid looked at him long and hard, trying
to judge just how serious his "maybe" was.
Her look softened, and she reached for his
hand. He snatched it away from her and
pushed himself out of his chair, going to stare
out the back window.

"You've known each other only a matter of
days," she said gently.

"Excuse me. Did I say this made sense?" he
asked sardonically, his brows lifting in exaggerated question. "I don't recall saying that,
but as long as we're on the subject, *how* long
did you know John before you were certain
you wanted to marry him?"

Ingrid sighed, planting her elbows on the table and rubbing two fingers to each temple.
Everyone who knew her knew the story of how
she and John had met on a casual double date
while paired up with other people. She swore
up and down she had known by the time they
left the restaurant John Wood was the man she
wanted to marry. "Point taken," she said wearily.

"Maybe you don't think I'm capable of that
kind of depth of feeling," Matt said, continuing
on the defensive, his tone particularly cutting
because the doubts he was expressing on his

sister's behalf were doubts he'd had about himself. "Maybe you think I was just going to go through my whole life married to my career, fooling around on the side with women who didn't expect any kind of commitment from me."

Ingrid gave him a furious look and slapped her hand down on the table. "Stop it!" she snapped. "Will you just listen to me for two minutes?"

He checked his watch just to needle her and gazed off into the middle distance, waiting.

"Matt, she's Amish. Do you have any idea what that means?"

"She dresses funny and drives a horse."

"Don't be smart. Do you know anything about the Amish way of life?"

He gave a belligerent shrug. "It's Sarah's religion. That's fine. It doesn't matter. I don't care. We can work around that."

"It *does* matter," Ingrid insisted. "The Amish here are from the Old Order. They're very strict in their beliefs, particularly as separatists. Sarah is walking a fine line just by working here. Do you know what would happen to her if they found out she was involved with a Yankee?"

"I'm sure you're going to tell me," he said, making clear that he didn't want to hear it.

Ingrid went on just the same, bound by a duty to her friend and her brother. "It's called the *Meidung*. Unless she repented publicly, she would be ostracized, shunned by her people. They wouldn't be allowed to acknowledge her in any way. They wouldn't be able to speak to her or take something from her hand or sit at a dinner table with her. She would lose everything—her faith, her family."

"You're making this up," Matt said angrily, knowing he sounded utterly childish.

"I'm not," Ingrid replied calmly.

"That's barbaric."

"It's their way, and they have their reasons for it."

Matt leaned against the window frame and stared out at the farmyard cast in bronze by the late afternoon sun. Sarah was bent over by the barn door, pouring out milk for an assortment of cats. He thought of the way she had spoken of her family, the love that had lit her eyes. He thought of her relationship with little Jacob. Would she be willing to give all that up? Did he have the right to ask her? Was he insane to even consider it?

They'd only known each other a matter of days. But now he'd fallen in love with her in those few days. He'd never felt anything like it. It was powerful and consuming and he couldn't imagine it ever burning out. And it wasn't just lust. He knew lust. Lust didn't have anything to do with the way he felt when he watched Sarah open a book and become in-

stantly absorbed in the process of learning.
Lust didn't make him want to protect her and
defend her. It wasn't lust that ached when he
saw her tears. This was love, the real McCoy.
Just because it had struck like a bolt of lightning out of the blue didn't make it any less
real.

He was in love with Sarah Troyer. And now
Ingrid was telling him it was against the rules,
rules he hadn't even known existed. The sudden knowledge of the stakes and the penalties
sent him reeling.

Why hadn't Sarah warned him? Why hadn't
she told him this?

"I don't want to see you hurt, either, Matt."
Ingrid had come to stand opposite him, mir-
roring his stance, her shoulder against the
white-painted frame of the window. The look
he gave her was bleak, and her heart nearly
broke. "Oh, Matt," she whispered, hugging
herself against an inner chill. "You really are
in love with her, aren't you? Of all the women
who've fallen in love with you, you have to
want the one you can't have."

He was thinking something along the same
lines himself. Anger swelled inside him like a
balloon, crowding his chest, making it difficult
to breathe. Anger at the injustice of it and anger at Sarah. She had let him get in too deep
to save himself, and now he was being thrown
an anvil. Why would she do that unless her

feelings for him didn't run as deeply as she'd professed?

She'd been playing with him. It seemed impossible, yet, at the same time, it seemed the only answer. And he'd thought she was the one who needed protecting! He'd thought she was the naive one. He suddenly felt as if he'd been played for a colossal fool.

In one lithe, violent motion he turned and slammed his fist against the window frame, rattling the glass panes. Without a word to his sister, he stormed out of the house, limping heavily as he crossed the yard going in search of Sarah.

He found her behind the barn dumping a bale of hay into the ring of an old tractor tire that lay on the ground. Her horse looked up from his dinner and pricked his ears, snorting at the sight of Matt as if he could sense the anger that rolled off the man like steam. Sarah glanced up, her eyes widening. She barely had time to straighten before Matt had her by the shoulders.

He gave her a shake and hauled her up against him, making her bend backward as he leaned over her. His face was a mask of fury. "Why didn't you tell me?" he demanded.

"T-tell you what?" she asked, every warning system in her body going on red alert. He was frightening her. Her sweet, gentle Matt was frightening her. The idea itself was enough to make her tremble.

"Dammit, Sarah," he shouted. "Why didn't you warn me?"

"Matt!" she cried, twisting in his grasp. "Stop it! You're hurting me!"

"Oh yeah? Well, how do you think I feel right now? I've just been informed that if you're caught consorting with me, you'll be considered a pariah and cast out of your society. Why the hell didn't you warn me, Sarah?"

She looked up at him with bleak eyes, the fear instantly gone and sadness filling up the space inside her. "Would it have mattered?"

"Yes!" He released her abruptly and stepped back, squeezing his eyes shut and raking his hands through his hair as pain and confusion twisted inside him. "No . . . I don't know."

His last words came out on a strained, tired whisper. What would he have done differently? Would he have stayed away from her from the start? Could he really have prevented himself from falling in love with her?

"What difference will it make to you?" she asked quietly. "You're from a different world. You will go back to that world because it's where you belong."

"Oh, I see," Matt said sarcastically, letting his pain goad him. "You just wanted a little fling. I looked like a nice, safe guy to have a little adventure with, right? You took one look at me and figured I'd never stick around—"

"No!"

"What? Have I got the word 'fickle' tattooed on my body somewhere or something?" he asked, forcing a dry laugh.

"No!" Sarah said, miserable. She could barely look him in the eye. A little adventure was exactly what she had wanted. She hadn't bargained on getting so much more. She had certainly never considered that Matt would end up getting hurt. All along she'd thought only her own heart had been at risk. "I never counted on falling in love with you."

"You just wanted to sleep with me," he said, the bitterness in his tone as caustic as acid.

Sarah reacted without thinking, slapping his face hard. "How dare you," she said, her voice trembling just above a whisper. "How dare you say such a thing to me."

She turned away from him and through her tears stared at the hand she'd struck him with. Never in her life had she raised a hand to anybody. Now in anger she'd hit the man she loved. Shame throbbed inside her in a physical ache. Shame and despair and heartache. She ran for the relative darkness of the barn, stopping just inside the door, welcoming the coolness and the absence of bright light. For a moment she just let those things absorb her. She breathed in the sweet scent of hay and the mustiness of cobwebs. She listened to two cats playing in the straw of Otis's stall.

"Sarah?" Matt's voice came to her through the haze of her suffering, sounding higher than normal and strained. He cleared his throat and shuffled his feet on the cracked concrete of the barn floor. "Sarah, I'm sorry." He sniffed and cleared his throat again. "I shouldn't have said that."

"I came to you out of love," she whispered, tears spilling past the barrier of her lashes and rolling down her cheeks.

"I know. I know you did," he murmured, hurting more from the pain he'd inflicted on her than from anything she had done to him.

Trembling, he slid his arms around her and pulled her back against him. He brushed his cheek against the top of her head, encountering the stiff gauze of her *kapp* rather than the softness of her hair; the barrier of her Amishness in a tangible form. He wanted to tear it off and throw it aside, and at the same time he called himself a hypocrite. Wasn't it her Amishness that had first drawn him to her—her simplicity, her naiveté, her sweet nature? He couldn't both change her and have her remain the same.

"I wanted to know what it was to be in love," she said. "Was that so wrong of me? I knew in the end you would go back to the city and I would be left here to my life, but I fell in love with you. Was it so wrong of me to want to hold on to that for a little while?"

"No."

"I don't think there can be sin in loving someone," she said shakily. "Only joy and pain."

Blinking against the sting of his own tears, Matt turned her in his arms and held her close. Love, the most complex of emotions. Sarah had reduced it down to its simplest elements: A time of joy and a time of pain. Was that really all they were to be allowed? It seemed so little when he had waited so long. He wondered if Sarah felt as cheated as he did. She sounded resigned. He would go back to "the world" and she would remain here, and their love would fade into pain, then into memories. He ached with emptiness just thinking about it. That was the way it would be, though. Even as he wondered if she would go with him if he asked, he knew her answer. She had already given it to him. She wouldn't leave her way of life, wouldn't leave her family.

"What happens now?" he asked. "I don't want to get you in trouble with your people."

Sarah felt her heart crack. What had she expected him to say? Had she really expected him to ask her for a future? He couldn't change who he was and, no matter how often she had dreamed of it, she couldn't either. There was her family to consider. She couldn't

shame them, couldn't leave them. The thought
of never seeing them again tore her apart.
Then there was the world to consider. What
would the big world do with the like of her?
She had seen the way it had battered Matt. It
would chew her up and spit her out. Matt
would tire of her eventually; her novelty would
wear off. He was quick to defend her now, but
the fact of the matter was she would likely em-
barrass him if she were transplanted into his
world.

No. She'd known all along what they had
was this time, the here and now.

"No one knows about us," she said, hating
the need to hide their love. "What we have between us is ours alone. I don't want to give it
up, not until I have to."

Matt tightened his arms around her. "Me
neither."

He wanted to cling to her every minute they
had left. He wanted to store up the feel of her
and the taste of her and her sweet scent so
that when the end came he would have something to take with him. The injured pride that
prodded at him to walk away couldn't hold a
candle to his desperate need to take as much
love as Sarah would give him.

He turned her in his arms and bent to kiss
her. Sarah met him halfway, just as hungry to
gather memories, to stockpile them for the
long nights ahead when all they would have

was longing for a touch, the memory of a kiss, the ache of a missing corner of a heart. Their mouths clashed and dueled greedily, insatiably. Each framed the other's face with trembling hands, trying to memorize the texture of skin, the angle of bones. They took deep, thirsty kisses, drinking in flavors and feelings and each other's tears, and heat flared through them in the flash fire of sudden and desperate passion.

Matt tore his mouth away and crushed her against him in an embrace that attempted to imprint his body with the outline of hers. His gaze settled on the bales of hay stacked in tiers beside the aisle and on the heavy woolen horse rug that lay folded over the door of a stall. Within minutes they had the rug spread on a wide flat section of bales and they knelt facing each other, snatching kisses and unfastening buttons.

Too eager to go through the process of undressing, they merely uncovered essential areas. Matt's shirt fell open so Sarah could stroke her hands over the hard panes of his chest and tease his flat nipples through the fine dusting of curling black hair. The bodice of her dress fell down around her hips, baring her breasts for his gaze and touch.

Carefully, he lay her down on their makeshift bed, his mouth trailing reverent kisses from her mouth to her throat to her collar-

bone, savoring every delectable inch of her.
When his lips, warm and wet, closed over her
nipple, she let out a sound of desperation. Her
fingers tangled in his short, thick hair, pressing him closer, urging him to nuzzle and
nurse.

After a long moment he raised his head just
enough to study the sweet bud of flesh, watching it pucker as the air cooled the heat his
mouth had generated. He brushed a thumb
across the distended peak, wringing a gasp
from her and causing her to arch against the
pressure of the hard thigh he had wedged between her legs. Then he bent to the task of giving her other breast equal treatment, sucking,
nibbling, laving her nipple with his tongue,
relishing the sweet taste of her and the way
she offered herself to him with nothing held
back. He took what she yielded, seeking to satisfy his own selfish needs and to give her all
that was in his heart, as well.

Settling his mouth on hers once again, he
knelt between her legs and worked the fly of
his pants with fingers that fumbled in their
hurry. Breaking the kiss, Sarah reached between them and did the work herself, popping
the button and easing the zipper down. She
took him into her hand, her fingers tracing the
hard length of him, testing the weight, closing
around the heat. She stroked him and guided

him toward her, lifting her hips and opening herself to him.

Matt slid into her on one slow stroke. A shuddering sigh slipped from his lips to hers as her tight, warm woman's pocket enveloped him, welcoming him into her body.

"I do love you, Sarah," he said on the softest of whispers.

"I know," she answered, though her heart throbbed with sadness at the knowledge that the love he was willing to give could never be enough, that their worlds would eventually pull them apart.

But for now, for this achingly tender moment, they were together. They were as close as two souls could be. If this was all they were to be allowed, then at least she had the knowledge that this was perfect. She had never felt more womanly, more cherished, more loved than she did in that moment, sharing herself with the man of her heart.

They moved together, the desire to prolong the moment overrun by the urgency to take everything they could while they had the chance. Matt clutched her to him, his arms around her shoulders as he thrust and withdrew. Sarah clung to him, wrapping herself around him, her hands pressed to he straining muscles of his back, her legs wrapped tightly around his hips as if she intended to hold him within her forever.

The end came for Sarah first. It was an explosion of feeling that for a long moment blotted out all else. Matt felt her stiffen in his arms, then groaned as her inner contractions tugged him, luring his body toward the same sweet oblivion. He forced himself to hold back, ruthlessly checking his own desires as he moved into her again and again, prolonging Sarah's climax and building it into a second shattering burst. This time when she cried out, his voice joined hers as he let go of his control and surrendered himself to the bliss of completion.

As they walked back to the house the sun was just slipping past the horizon in a blaze of orange so intense, the countryside was drenched in color—the farm buildings, the cornstalks, the thin blond weeds that waved along the edge of the road. Silhouetted against the vibrant sky a V formation of Canada geese flew south, their mournful honking sounding the way. Daylight gave way to dusk. The sun snuck away, leaving the air crisp with the promise of a hard frost.

Matt took Sarah's hand as they walked. They moved slowly because neither wanted to leave their closeness behind and because Matt was suddenly feeling his injuries, both physical and emotional. He limped toward the back of the big farmhouse, feeling worn-out and battered, once again without hope. Neither of them voiced the question that was uppermost in their minds—how much time did they have left together?

As they approached the foot of the back porch steps the screen door swung open and the answer to their question stared them in the face. Their time was up. Isaac Maust had come to fetch his daughter home.

10

Sarah took one look at her father's face and stopped in her tracks at the bottom of the steps. The fury and condemnation in his eyes stung like a slap across the face. She let go of Matt's hand, then had to endure his look of hurt as well as her own feelings of guilt.

"Pop," she said quietly, not quite able to ask why he had come. She didn't want to know.

Isaac stared down at her with a thunderous scowl, drawing his beetle brows together and carving deep brackets beside his mouth. He spoke to her in harsh German. "Are you a daughter of mine, Sarah Troyer, that you would shame me so?"

Sarah's eyes flooded, but she refused to let a single tear fall. Old wounds cracked open inside her. He had never understood her, had never tried to. All her life he had disapproved of her spirit, her hunger for learning, the insatiable yearning for something she couldn't define. He had never taken the time to understand how hard she'd tried to be the kind of daughter he wanted.

"Do you ask or do you accuse?" she said, meeting his hard gaze head-on.

Isaac left the question unanswered, ignoring her as if he didn't understand the language she spoke. His gaze raked down over Matt with contempt. "Is this how the English have you care for their guests? This holding of the hands and walking with a man who is not your husband nor even of your faith?"

Sarah turned his own tactic around on him, refusing to answer. Beside her, Matt shuffled his feet restlessly, planting his hands on his lean hips.

"What's he saying?" he asked, his gaze shifting uneasily back and forth between the old man and Sarah. He could sense the tension and he didn't like it. He especially didn't like the tears welling in Sarah's eyes. That alone stirred dislike for her father inside him. "What does he want?"

"Why have you come here, Pop?" she asked in English. As much as she didn't want to hear this in any language, it wasn't right to force Matt to wonder what was going on.

Naturally, Isaac didn't agree. He went on speaking in the guttural dialect out of stubbornness more than habit, she suspected. "There is family business. You are needed at home. Come and pack your things."

"What family business? Why am I needed? Is Mom ill?" Sarah asked, concern for her family overriding all else. Wringing her hands nervously, she moved closer to the steps to get a better look at her father's impassive face. "What's wrong?"

"Plenty is wrong. We had visitors today. First, Micah Hochstetler, then the deacon."

Sarah felt a deep chill settle in her bones at the mention of the deacon. If her father was there because the deacon had come, then it hadn't been a social call; it had to do with her. It was the deacon's duty to approach any member of the community suspected of disobeying the *Ordnung*, the rules of the church. Deacon Lapp was a close friend of Isaac. He would have gone to Isaac first in any matter concerning one of the Maust children. What she didn't know, what she was afraid to know, was what the concern might be about.

"I've spoken with Deacon Lapp and also with the bishop about my job here," she said, grasping desperately for what she hoped was the root of the trouble. "They said I could—"

"This isn't to do with the work," Isaac interrupted. His face grew dark and his hand trembled as he raised it and pointed a gnarled finger at Matt. "This is to do with this Yankee."

"Whoa, wait a minute here!" Matt protested angrily, bringing his hands up in front of him to halt Isaac's verbal assault. "I may not speak the lingo here, but I think I know when I'm being insulted."

"Insults?" Isaac said, finally consenting to using English. "You speak to me of insults when you shame my daughter before God and her people?"

The look in Matt's eyes hardened to something like hatred. He stared at Isaac Maust and saw the personification of what would forever keep him from the only woman he'd ever loved. He cherished Sarah with everything that was in his heart. To have that love sullied by accusation was something he wasn't going to stand still for, and it didn't matter if the accuser was Sarah's father or God himself.

"Sarah hasn't done anything to be ashamed of. Your daughter is a bright, vibrant, loving young woman. I happen to care for her very deeply."

"What has Micah Hochstetler to do with this?" Sarah asked, jumping in as quickly as she could to derail her father from the train of conversation Matt had started on. She didn't know yet what damage had been done or what the deacon had had to say, but she didn't want the hole to get dug any deeper.

Her father turned to her with a sour expression. "As he was driving past here yesterday with a load of corn he saw you out on the lawn chasing around with this Englishman, behav-

ing wild, your hair loose and down for all to
see. Do you deny this?"

For an instant Sarah had the wild urge to
make up a story that might excuse what her
father's neighbor had seen, but none come to
mind, and she only felt wretched for even
thinking it. How could she consider degrading
the love she felt for Matt just for the sake of
placating her father? What kind of coward was
she?

"Do you deny it?" Isaac demanded again,
coming down a step to loom over his daughter
like a righteous judge. The breeze caught the
ends of his beard, and the porch light backlit
him like a holy aura, making him look as for-
midable as Moses on the mountain. "Do you
deny it?"

"Do you ask for an explanation?" Sarah
questioned softly, tears crowding her throat.
"Do you give me any benefit of doubt?"

"Do you deserve it?"

That wasn't the point, Sarah thought sadly,
but she didn't waste her breath saying it. Isaac
wouldn't hear her. She looked away from him,
tears sliding down her cheeks, hurting too
badly to go on looking for some hint of approval or understanding or even compassion
from him. Her father was a hard man, unyield-
ing, severe. He loved his family, but he toler-
ated nothing save absolute obedience. Pity she

had been born as stubborn as he was and with a spirit that defied authority at most turns.

"Go and pack your things," he said, his voice thick with disgust and disapproval.

Sarah's first instinct was to defy him, but she thought of her mother and her family, especially Jacob, and curbed her rebellion. In that moment she didn't care how Isaac might suffer from her disobedience, but she couldn't cause the rest of her family undue anxiety just for the sake of spite. Besides, if it were possible for the trouble to be cleared up by a simple visit to her home for a few days and perhaps an earnest talk with some of the church elders, then she knew she had best take the opportunity and save them all a lot of pain.

She moved toward the steps, but Matt reached out and stopped her with a hand on her arm.

"Wait a second," he said, glaring at Isaac. "This isn't Sarah's fault. I didn't know it was against her religion to have fun. I was just teasing her. It was harmless."

"Was it?" Isaac said, his gaze going meaningfully to the hand Matt had unconsciously settled on Sarah's arm. "Let me tell you something, Mister English," he said, wagging a finger in Matt's face. "You may not know our ways, but Sarah knows them well. It is for her to resist the temptations of the world and when she don't, it is for her to atone for her sins."

"She hasn't committed any sins!"

Isaac gave a snort and took hold of his daughter's other arm. "That is sure not for you to decide."

"And it is for you?" Matt questioned angrily. His grip tightened on Sarah's arm. "Who do you think you are? God?"

Isaac's weathered face colored deeply. "I am not God," he hissed. "I am God's servant. I obey his laws." He tried to jerk Sarah toward him, but Matt held fast.

"You obey your own laws," Matt sneered. "Sarah isn't guilty of anything but being in love. That might be a sin in your eyes, but I doubt it is in God's."

"Love." Isaac spat out the word as if it made a foul taste in his mouth. "I know of your kind of love, Englishman. Love of the flesh. Have you defiled my daughter so?"

A red mist washed before Matt's eyes. It was all he could do to not let got of Sarah and take a swing at her father. His muscles tensed to the hardness of granite, his left hand clenched into a fist, but something told him his most important priority was holding on to Sarah, so he clung to the leash of his temper as he clung to the woman beside him.

"I've never *defiled* anyone," he said, his tone dangerously low and thrumming with fury.

Isaac looked away from him, pinning Sarah with his gaze instead. "He speaks of your love, daughter," he said, reverting to German once again. "Are your sins even more terrible than I thought? More terrible than anyone knows?"

Once again Sarah refused to answer. She wouldn't soil what she had shared with Matt in love by calling it a sin. It wasn't a sin in her heart. Her soul was twined with Matt's more closely than it had been with her own husband's. She was married to him in her own eyes and, she prayed, in the eyes of God. She lifted her chin, winning her another black mark in her father's eyes.

"You have lain with this English?" he said, his voice shaking with anger. His fierce grip tightened on her arm, and she had to grit her teeth to keep from wincing. "You are a fornicator? A whore?"

She bit her lip to keep from saying anything at all. She knew she should have bowed her head. Expressing shame and humility might have won her some mercy, but she wasn't ashamed and she wouldn't pretend it. She looked at her father squarely and let him see her defiance, let him see the rebellion she had held inside for so long. She raised her chin another notch in pride, which was itself a sin.

Isaac cursed her, an expression of pure rage twisting his features. His right hand lashed out like a bolt of lightning and caught Sarah

across the mouth, splitting her lip. The force
of the blow turned her head and burned her
cheek, but still she refused to cry.

Matt jerked her back out of Isaac's grasp,
swearing viciously under his breath. He turned
her to survey the damage her father had done,
cradling her face gently in his trembling
hands. He wiped a bead of blood from her lip
with his thumb, fighting the urge to kiss it
away.

"I'll be all right," she whispered, her eyes
huge with pleading. "Please, Matt, don't make
it worse."

"How the hell could I make it any worse
than this?" he asked, his voice shaking. He
looked up at Isaac with loathing. "You pack
quite a punch for a pacifist. Get out of here.
Nobody abuses women in front of me, no matter how righteous and pious they think they
are. Leave. Now."

"Come, Sarah," Isaac commanded as if she
were a dog to be ordered about. He showed no
open remorse for what he'd done, but his expression had been wiped clean of anger and
rage and was now blank.

Sarah started toward him, and again Matt
held her back.

"Matt," she said softly, glancing up at him.
"It's all right."

His eyes widened incredulously. "It's not all
right! You're a grown woman. He can't come

here and knock you around and drag you off by the hair! He doesn't have any say in your life."

"He is my father."

"That doesn't give him the right—"

"Matt." Ingrid's voice drew his attention to the porch, where his sister had come to stand in the open doorway with her basset hound on her feet, and her arms crossed against the chill of the early evening. Her expression was both strained and guarded as she looked at him. "Let it go. Sarah knows what she's doing."

He worked his jaw, fighting the urge to argue with her. Deep inside he couldn't escape the feeling that he was Sarah's protector, her knight in shining armor ready to slay any dragon for her. Some protector, he thought derisively. It was because of him her father had been driven to strike her. It was because of him she may be in serious trouble with her people. Once again he had managed to hurt her when his greatest desire was to love her and keep her from harm. Maybe she was right in saying he should go back to his world. It was becoming painfully clear that their separate worlds couldn't mix.

"Please, Matt," she whispered tremulously, tears spilling past her lashes and down her cheeks. "Please."

She was asking him to let her go. She'd told him she'd known all along their time together would be brief. He had fought the idea just as he had wanted to fight any threat to Sarah herself. He wanted to fight it still, but she was asking him to let go. If he followed his heart and fought for her, he would only end up destroying her. The selfish man inside him argued that they would still have each other and the love that had blossomed so quickly and so brilliantly between them. But he knew deep down that the cost would be too great. He couldn't force her to change, couldn't ask her to give up her family and her faith and her way of life. She wasn't willing to make that sacrifice for him and if he forced her to, how could their love possibly survive?

It took a terrible effort, but he pulled his hand away from Sarah's arm and stepped back, conceding the battle to Isaac Maust. Sarah looked up at him with an expression that tore his heart in two.

"I'm sorry," she said, the words barely audible. "I'm so sorry I hurt you."

Matt felt the pressure of tears behind his own eyes as he looked at her, committing to memory her every feature. He reached out and brushed a drop of moisture from the crest of her cheek. "Just don't be sorry you loved me," he said, then turned and walked away, limping heavily and feeling old and beaten.

•   •   •

She was gone in a matter of minutes. Matt sat on a decorative iron bench beneath a maple tree on the far side of the yard and watched the black buggy pull out, white reflective tape glowing eerily in the dark as it made its way down the road. The last rays of the sunset had faded to black, a color appropriate for mourning, Matt thought. He looked out at the millions of stars that dotted the sky like fairy dust, his gaze fastening on the brightest.

Star light, star bright, first star I see tonight . . .

He shook his head in amazement at the nursery rhyme that had popped into his head. He hadn't experienced a sense of wonder in a long, long time. For months now he'd felt as aged and cynical as the world itself—until Sarah had come into his life. In her quiet way she had awakened in him an appreciation for the simple beauty of the world around him. Now she was gone and all the joy of that beauty had gone with her.

Blossom came trotting across the yard, nose to the ground. She made a beeline to him, sniffed his shoes, and plopped down in front of him. Her somber, woebegone expression was clear to him thanks to the faint silver glow of the yard light that stood between the house and the barn.

"I feel worse than you look," he murmured.

The hound whined and lay her head on her paws in apparent sympathy.

Ingrid emerged from the shadows of the house and came to sit beside him on the bench with his leather jacket draped across her lap.

"You shouldn't let yourself get a chill, Dr. Thorne," she said with absolutely no censure in her voice.

Matt didn't take the jacket, nor did he say anything for a long while. He just sat there absorbing his sister's silent comfort, staring out at the night and marveling at the quiet of it.

"Do you think she'll make them understand?" he asked.

"I don't know. They'll forgive her if she asks for it. They're very forgiving people."

"What about that thing you told me, that mide thing."

"The *Meidung*. Shunning is serious business for the unrepentant. It might not come to that. Like I said, they're gentle, forgiving people."

Matt gave a harsh laugh. "Her father doesn't seem very forgiving."

"Isaac is a hard man, almost bitter for some reason. He's very strong in the *Unserem Weg*, the old ways. Very strict."

"I could have killed him for hitting her."

"I know."

They sat in silence for another few minutes. Ingrid leaned over and rested her head on his shoulder. She took one of his hands in hers and squeezed it tight. "I'm sorry, Matt."

So am I, he thought, hurting in a way no drug could ease.

"Is there anything I can do to help her?" he asked.

"Stay out of it. They won't tolerate interference, especially not from you. Make a clean break. Get on with your life."

What life? a lonely voice asked inside him.

Realistically, he knew he would take Ingrid's advice. Realistically, he knew he would go back to work, and in a few months his brief stay here and his brief affair with a young Amish woman would be a memory, the awful pain dulled by the anesthetic effects of time. Realistically, he knew all of these things, but in his heart he couldn't accept any of it at the moment. In his heart he knew only that he'd found something bright and pure that had lighted his life when everything had seemed bleak and dingy, and now that special something had been snatched away from him, wrenched from his grasp even sooner than he had feared. In his heart he knew only that he felt more alone than he had ever felt before.

He wondered if Sarah was feeling the same way.

He looked out at the starlit sky and listened

to the breeze rattle the skeletal cornstalks and the dried leaves in the trees. He felt the autumn chill bite into his bones, and he thought about Sarah in the house down the road.

Don't be sorry you loved me. . . .

11

"Deacon Lapp suggested a visit to the Ohio relatives," Isaac said. "A period for you to pray and reflect, to heal the soul."

As if her love for Matt were an illness she could recuperate from given some time in a sterile environment, Sarah thought bitterly. They sat at her mother's round oak kitchen table, Isaac and Anna Maust and herself. The rest of the family had been sent to bed with no explanation of what was going on or why Sarah was home. It seemed quite clear to one and all it was not a joyous occasion. The talk going on in the kitchen by the light of the kerosene lamps was serious stuff.

"No confession?" Sarah asked. She felt numb and it had nothing to do with the buggy ride home into the chill of the October wind.

"He knows only of what Micah Hochstetler told him, and he tends to be lenient toward you for some reason I cannot fathom. Time away to clear your head of foolishness, he thinks, and I say we send you before things get worse. I won't have you disgrace my family."

My family, as if she were not a part of it, as if he had already shunned her himself. The remark cut, but Sarah didn't let it show. She gave him a long look of contempt for his hypocrisy. He could call her a harlot and a sinner, but God forbid anyone else should find out. Were her supposed sins any less because he was the only one who knew of them? As righteous as Isaac pretended to be, Sarah thought he should have gone ahead and reported her to the bishop. Isaac would no doubt have taken great delight in her excommunication if not for the fact that it would reflect badly on him.

She looked at her mother, knowing Anna Maust would not argue with her husband on this point or any other. Plump and still blond, more than ten years her husband's junior, Anna Maust had ever been the quiet, dutiful wife. She was a woman with a kind heart and a soft touch, who had always looked on her eldest daughter's restless spirit with a kind of puzzled awe. She looked at Sarah now with sad blue eyes and said, "It is for the best, Sarah. *Es waar Gotters Wille.*"

It is God's will. Her mother had said that same thing to her when her baby had died of pneumonia and when Samuel had been killed. Every terrible thing that happened, Anna heaped the blame on God's doorstep.

"No," Sarah said quietly, rising from her chair. "It is Isaac Maust's will."

She expected an explosion from Isaac, but none came.

"Tomorrow I will see to the getting of the bus ticket," he said.

Sarah gave no indication she had heard him. She turned and left the kitchen, making her way upstairs toward the tiny bedroom she used when she was home. On her way down the hall she stopped at Jacob's door and looked in on him. He was asleep but terribly restless, tossing and turning, groaning a little in his sleep.

"He snuck too many pieces of apple strudel last night," Anna whispered, coming up close beside her daughter. "He suffered for it today, but I gave him a good big dose of castor oil. He will be better by morning."

Sarah watched her baby brother for another long moment, feeling apprehension stir in the pit of her stomach. She hated seeing Jacob ill. It frightened her. And the thought of leaving him in a few days tightened her apprehension into a knot.

"To bed now with you, Sarah," her mother said, pulling Jacob's door shut. "This day has been too long. I am wanting another sunrise to brighten things."

Sarah turned toward her mother and said, "In my heart there will be no sunrise."

Anna was quiet for a moment, lost in thought. "Did you love him so much, this Englishman?" she asked at last, her voice soft and wistful.

"Yes."

Anna closed her eyes and bowed her head, as if in fervent prayer, then squeezed her daughter's hands and bid her a whispered good night.

By morning Jacob was no better. Anna bundled him up and rode with Isaac into Jesse, where she took the boy to see Dr. Coswell while Isaac made his pilgrimage to the bus depot. The doctor casually pronounced Jacob's malady as a case of the flu that was currently going around and sent him home.

Sarah spent the morning packing her things for her trip, carefully folding her dresses and aprons and underthings. As a gesture of pure rebellion, she packed her *Glamour* magazine and her bottle of *Evening in Paris* perfume. Throughout the process she kept thinking that she didn't want to go. She wanted to go back down the road to Thornewood and to Matt, but she knew better. Matt had never suggested they had a future together. She had given herself to him in love, knowing in the end they would part. And she had to think of her family, of her mother and her sister Ruth and her brothers and Jacob. She had remained in the faith because of them, because she loved them.

It was for their sakes she would go to Ohio to stay with relatives she barely knew.

In the afternoon she helped shuck corn until her thumbs were blistered, then helped prepare the evening meal for the family. No one had much to say to her. Even her brother Lucas, who at seventeen had honed teasing to a fine art, was unusually quiet. Isaac said nothing at all once he had announced she would be on the eight o'clock bus day after tomorrow. Her mother was full of worried and sympathetic looks, but short on words of comfort beyond her usual *Es waar Gotters Wille.*

Sarah kept her chin up and her mouth shut. She thought of Matt every single moment. She had never in her worst nightmares imagined it would hurt this much to leave him. After all, she had known the end would come eventually; she had been prepared for it from the first. But the ache gnawed at her incessantly, and she wondered vaguely if it were possible to die of such a pain.

When the dishes had been done and everyone else had settled into the living room to read or sew, she sought the one person in her life who had a chance of easing her suffering just by smiling at her—Jacob. He had had a miserable day of sickness and fitful sleep. As Sarah let herself into his room he moaned and kicked the quilt that covered him.

Sarah lit a lamp on the simple bedside table

and settled herself on the narrow bed, bending over her little brother and brushing back damp strands of blond hair from his forehead. He was burning up with fever. That alone was enough to put her heart in her throat, but when Jacob clutched his stomach and moaned, her worry soared to near the panic margin.

"Shhh . . . rest, *bobbli*," she whispered, trying to soothe both him and herself.

"Sarah?" Jacob called out weakly. "Sarah, it hurts me too much."

"What hurts?"

He didn't answer her but clutched his stomach and started to cry. Sarah bit her lip until she tasted blood, desperate to help Jacob, but uncertain of what she could do. He seemed much more ill than Dr. Coswell had diagnosed. Dr. Coswell, the man Matt had said wasn't fit to practice medicine on monkeys. What if the man had been wrong about Jacob? What if the boy had something that could threaten his life? She couldn't bear to lose Jacob!

In a panic she flew down the stairs and through the living room, saying nothing to anyone, registering their shocked looks only in the nether reaches of her mind. At the back door she paused only long enough to grab her cloak off its peg, then she was gone.

•   •   •

"She's being sent to Ohio to stay with relatives for a while," Ingrid said, slipping into the armchair catty-corner from Matt. They were in the library. The stereo hummed in the background. Matt had wedged himself into a corner of the sofa he had once shared with Sarah, sitting stiffly, riffling through the Minneapolis paper. He scowled and turned a page, cracking it like a whip, glanced over the columns without reading, turned a page, snapped it open with a flick of his wrists.

"No word of excommunication."

"Good news travels fast," he said sarcastically.

Ingrid ran a hand through her short dark hair and sighed. "I just heard via the grapevine. Isaac purchased a bus ticket this morning."

Matt nodded curtly, not looking up, though he wasn't taking in a single word of print. His first thought was to ask when Sarah was leaving, but he stifled it ruthlessly with common sense. It was over. There was no point in trying to see her again. She didn't love him enough to leave her folk and he loved her too much to ask. Time for any smart bachelor to cut bait and run. Actually, it was past time for that. He never should have let himself get so involved in the first place. But he'd been so in need of something, anything that would help life make sense again, and there had been

Sarah, the embodiment of everything he thought had gone out of life—goodness, innocence, faith.

Maybe Julia had been right. Maybe he had been trying to compensate. Maybe he had been trying to withdraw from the world, wrapping himself in the cocoon of Sarah Troyer's homemade skirts.

"I'll be going back to the Cities at the end of the week," he announced.

Ingrid said nothing. She probably knew he was not well enough to return to work, but she also knew better than to protest.

Outside the wind howled and hurled rain against the panes of the bay window. In the snug warmth of the library, the Righteous Brothers sang the mournful opening bars of "Unchained Melody." Matt folded his *Star-Tribune* with quick jerky movements and hurled it across the room in a burst of temper. In the front hall, Blossom sent up a howl as someone began pounding on the door.

Ingrid had just pushed herself up out of her seat when Sarah came rushing into the library, looking like the headless horseman had chased her all the way to Thornewood. Her *kapp* was gone. Her hair hung loose in wet strings, and rainwater dripped off the end of her reddened nose. The heavy black cloak she wore smelled of wet wool and horses.

"Sarah!" Ingrid said on a gasp.

Sarah looked right past her, her terrified gaze focusing on Matt. "Matt!" she exclaimed, her eyes huge in a pale face. "It's Jacob. He's terribly ill. You have to come. Please say you'll come right away!"

"Of course, I'll come," he murmured, so stunned by her sudden appearance that he had yet to react.

"Now!" she insisted, flying across the room to grab his hand and pull him up off the couch. Her fingers were like icicles, wet and white and painfully cold. She tugged him like an anxious child, sobbing, teeth chattering. "There's no time to lose! I'm afraid. Oh, *mein Gott*, I'm so afraid he's going to die!"

She began crying then and Matt instinctively pulled her into his arms, offering her his warmth and strength for an instant . . . and his love. It poured out of him unchecked, and he squeezed her tightly, not caring that her cape was wet or that her hair was dripping on his cashmere sweater. The hurt he had been struggling with was instantly set aside, concern for Sarah and for Jacob overriding all else.

"Hush, sweetheart," he whispered, stroking a hand over the damp tangle of her hair. "Everything's gong to be all right. Tell me what happened."

"Jacob . . . he's ill. So hot . . . in such pain. I'm going to lose him," she whispered, trembling violently in Matt's arms. Her legs and arms ached from clinging to the back of the horse she had ridden there bareback, and now her knees threatened to give way beneath her. She was scared out of her wits thinking about Jacob, thinking about how they had waited too long to try to save her own little Peter. "Please, Matt," she sobbed, sagging against him. "He's going to die!"

"Nobody's going to die," Matt said firmly, standing her back from him. "Do you understand me, Sarah? Nobody's going to die." He grabbed the jacket Ingrid tossed him and shrugged into it, his eyes never leaving Sarah's. "Not as long as I can prevent it."

Ingrid drove because she knew the way and had experience driving on gravel. The horse Sarah had galloped to Thornewood on had been hastily locked in the barn. No time had been spared to see to the animal's needs because Jacob's life hung in the balance.

The trio burst in on the Maust family like marauders, flinging back the kitchen door and storming into the house in a swirl of rain and wind that made the lanterns flicker in protest. A stunned Isaac raced into the kitchen to meet them, his feet bare, his suspenders dangling.

"Sarah! What is the meaning of this?" he demanded in a thunderous voice. "Why do you bring these people into my home? How dare you—"

"I dare because Jacob is dying!" she shouted in his face.

"Nonsense! The boy has been to see a doctor—"

"I won't take the time to argue with you on that point, Mr. Maust," Matt said, shouldering his way past Sarah's father. "Sarah's word is good enough for me. Where's the boy?"

"Upstairs. Hurry!" Sarah shouted, well beyond the verge of hysteria. "Hurry!"

Ignoring the stunned faces of the rest of Sarah's family, Matt turned and took the stairs as fast as he could, blocking out his own pain with the need to get to Jacob as quickly as possible. Footsteps rumbled like thunder behind him. At the top of the stairs he hesitated, uncertain of which direction to go and Sarah nearly bowled him over, running into him and shoving him down the hall.

In Jacob's room, he set about the business of examining the boy as best he could without benefit of any of the tools of his trade. The old cool settled inside him. His hands were steady. His mind functioned with the flawless precision of a computer, absorbing information, analyzing it, considering and discarding options and answers. He rattled off questions in rapid succession.

"When did he first become ill? How long has his fever been this high? Is he taking any medications?"

Anna Maust answered him in a thin, trembling voice as she stood beside the bed looking down on her youngest with tear-filled, worried eyes.

"The doctor said flu is all it is," she murmured almost to herself. "He prescribed aspirin."

Matt didn't waste energy commenting on Coswell's diagnosis or on the idiocy of prescribing aspirin to a child with a high fever in view of the latest findings on the dangers of Reye's syndrome. He concentrated on Jacob, checking his pupils, feeling glands, running his sensitive hands gently over the boy's belly, frowning as his lightest touch brought groans of pain from Jacob.

Sarah fell to her knees beside the bed on the far side, sobbing, reaching out to touch the child she had always loved as her own. Ingrid and the rest of the Maust family stood back, watching, silent except for Isaac.

"We don't want you here, English," he hissed vehemently. "We have a doctor. Your interference—"

Matt straightened from the bed and wheeled on the man, his face a mask of stone. "My interference is going to save your son's life if we can get him to a hospital fast enough. His appendix is on the verge of rupturing."

Isaac Maust turned white, the seriousness of the situation penetrating his anger. He stared into Matt Thorne's eyes and saw nothing but the grim truth.

"What can we do?" he asked.

"Pray." Matt was already in motion.

There was no phone to call for an ambulance or time to wait for one. Jacob was wrapped in the blankets from his bed and carried out to the back of Ingrid's station wagon, where Matt and Sarah climbed in beside him. Ingrid dove behind the wheel and the elder Mausts settled in the backseat, slamming the doors as the car's wheels spun on the gravel driveway.

Jesse Community Hospital sat on the north edge of town, a modern U-shaped one-story structure of red brick that housed a nursing home in one wing and a small number of hospital beds in the other. There were no more than five cars in the lot. Ingrid halted the station wagon at the glass doors emblazoned with the word Emergency in red, and Matt led the way into the hospital with Jacob curling against him in his arms, the boy moaning and crying. Sarah ran beside him, her fist gripping the sleeve of Matt's leather jacket, tears streaming down her cheeks. The nurse on duty, a stout, middle-aged woman with a puffball of red hair and a name tag that proclaimed her to be Velma Johansen, R.N., rushed around from behind the desk to meet them.

"I'm Dr. Thorne from County General in Minneapolis," Matt announced in a voice that rang with authority. "We've got a boy here with an appendix that's just about ready to blow. I want him prepped for surgery *stat*. Where can I scrub?"

"Down that hall on the left, Doctor," Nurse Johansen answered efficiently, pointing with one hand and yanking a gurney away from the wall with the other. "I'll call the nurse-anesthetist. We'll have him ready for you as soon as possible."

"Make it sooner," Matt barked, bolting down the hall.

He nearly collided with Dr. Coswell as the older man stepped out of an office to see what all the shouting was about. Coswell hefted his bulk out of the way at the last instant, jerking his cigarette out of his mouth.

"Dr. Thorne! What brings you here?"

"I don't have time to chat, Coswell," Matt said, shrugging out of his jacket. "I've got an emergency appendectomy to perform."

"You can't just come in here and take over my hospital!" Coswell bellowed, incredulous.

Matt gave him a cool look. "Watch me."

"This is completely irregular!" Coswell exclaimed, his face turning an unhealthy shade of purple. "I won't stand for it!" he said, his smoker's cough choking off the end of his sentence.

"Yeah, well, I'll cut that kid open with a pocketknife before I let you get near him with a scalpel, so you'd better get used to the idea," Matt said. He left Coswell sputtering and went to ready himself to save Jacob Maust's life.

The wait seemed interminable. Sarah's parents sat on a low couch, huddling together under the glow of the fluorescent lights, offering one another quiet support. Sarah felt too frantic to sit and paced along the end of the waiting room with one arm wrapped around her midsection and her other hand pressed to her mouth to keep from crying out or screaming in frustration. Her hair still hung loose and she had made no effort to comb it, letting it dry in a wild tangle of waves that fell past her waist.

Ingrid got up to pace with her, putting an arm around Sarah's waist and leaning her head against the taller woman's shoulder. "Matt's a great doctor," she said softly. "And he's not just talented, he's as stubborn as a two-headed mule, to boot. He'll take care of Jacob."

"I know," Sarah murmured, hugging her friend. "I would trust him with my life."

Ingrid gave her a long, speculative look. "Would you?" she asked, and Sarah knew they were no longer speaking of Matt's abilities as a physician.

The question stopped her cold, but just as she started to ask Ingrid what she had meant, Matt emerged from a door at the end of the hall. He limped toward them looking tired and rumpled in baggy surgical greens. Lines of worry and concentration had etched themselves across his forehead and around his mouth, making him look ten years older. As he neared the waiting area he pulled his surgeon's cap off and mussed his hair with his hand. He stopped first to say a few words to Anna and Isaac, who listened intently, then bowed their heads in prayer, then he turned toward Sarah, his dark eyes fastening on hers.

"He's going to be fine," he said softly.

Her whole body shuddered with relief. She closed her eyes and said a quick prayer of thanks, then the tears started to flow. Without hesitating, she sought the refuge of Matt's embrace, pressing her cheek to his chest. He wrapped his arms around her and kissed her temple.

"It's all right, sweetheart," he whispered tenderly. "It's all right. Everything's going to be just fine."

He held her that way for a long while, not caring in the least that her parents were watching. If he couldn't have her forever, at least he could have her for now, and he could give her comfort if she wouldn't take his love.

"It's all right," he murmured, brushing his lips against her hair.

Sarah looked up at him and sniffed. "Thank you for saving him, Matt. I love him so much."

"I know."

"And I love you," Sarah whispered, lifting a hand to stroke her fingertips down his cheek.

But not as much, he thought sadly. Not enough.

Eventually he took them to see a groggy Jacob. While Sarah was busy fussing over her brother, Isaac drew Matt out into the dark hall.

"I've done you a disservice, Matt Thorne," Isaac said humbly. "You saved my son's life. For this I thank you."

"And for Sarah?" Matt asked, meeting the old man's gaze head-on.

"Let her go," Isaac said. There was no anger in his eyes now, only sadness and pleading. "She belongs with her people. You know nothing of our ways, nor she of your world."

"I love her."

"How can you love in so short a time? I think you cannot even know her."

"That's funny." Matt's mouth twisted into an ironic little smile that held no humor as he thought of Sarah with her hunger to learn and the inner fire she had yet to release. "I was just thinking the same thing about you. You've had her with you her whole life, and I don't think you know her at all."

"I know that she is Amish, as is her family."

Matt said nothing. He turned and looked into the room to see Sarah bent over her brother Jacob whom she loved like a son. She was smiling and teasing him, her face glowing. *I would have given her sons,* he thought, pain tightening its fist inside him. *I would have given her a family. I would have given her anything.*

But she hadn't asked.

He turned slowly then and walked away, wondering if the town of Jesse had a bar.

12 A shooting victim, an assault victim, a botched suicide, a bleeding ulcer, a dozen cases of the latest Asian flu strain, and a motorcyclist who hadn't had the foresight to put a helmet on before hurling himself into the side of a garbage truck. Just another day on the job.

Matt slumped onto the orange vinyl couch in the doctors' lounge, dropping his head down on the squeaky tufted arm. He was tired, but his fatigue didn't have anything to do with the hours he'd been working. This was a weariness that went deeper than his muscles and sank into the essence of his being. He'd been back in Minneapolis a week and on the job for four days. The chief of staff had protested his early return, but not with much sincerity. His life as Matt Thorne, head honcho of County General ER, had fallen quickly back into the routine he remembered.

Only he didn't remember it being so emotionally empty. He had never before met the flirtatious teasing of the female members of the staff with a complete lack of enthusiasm.

He didn't remember ever dreading going home to his apartment at night. He vaguely remembered charging at his job headfirst, but the man in those memories was a stranger to him. These days he operated on a kind of automatic pilot system—efficient and more than competent, but detached.

The city he had always loved and partaken of had lost some of its shine for him, as well. He found himself missing the rustle of cornstalks and the quiet of the country night. More than anything, he missed Sarah. Every time he thought of her riding on a bus full of strangers to Ohio his heart ached.

He had let her go and returned to "his world" only to find it wasn't the world he wanted to live in anymore. He had returned to his job because he was dedicated to helping and healing people, but this was no longer the way he wanted to go about it.

"Are you just resting or should I call the morgue?"

Julia flopped down into a chair of the same eye-burning orange vinyl as the couch and propped her big feet on a battle-scarred coffee table cluttered with old magazines and abandoned coffee cups. She wore the most relaxed version of "nursing whites" she could get away with—a lab jacket over an oversize T-shirt and baggy white sweatpants. Her wild red mane was more or less contained in a single long braid that hung over her shoulder like a length of rope.

"The jury's still out," Matt said. He pushed himself upright and mussed his hands through his hair, leaving it standing on end in tufts. "You want the truth, McCarver?"

"Always."

"I don't want to be here anymore."

"I know," she admitted quietly, picking at the end of her braid.

"It's not that I don't care," he went on. "It's just . . . I've done my tour of duty, that's all."

"I know."

He arched an eyebrow. "What? No fiery lecture on how needed I am?"

"No. This isn't the only place on earth that needs good doctors. You want the truth, Dr. T?"

"Usually."

Julia sat up and leaned forward, dangling her long hands between her knees. "I think I bugged you about coming back more because I missed my buddy than anything else, and now I feel like a guilty slug because you're miserable. I think maybe you'd better go back to that cornfield. You know in *Field of Dreams* it turned out to be heaven."

Matt made a face. "It wasn't heaven, it was Iowa."

"Oh, big deal." She scowled at him. "Don't

screw up my lines here, Thorne. I'm trying to tell you what you should do with your life."

"Pardon me."

"Go back, get married, be happy." She beat out the time of the sentence with one hand like a choir teacher.

"That sounds like a plan," Matt said with a sad smile. It was a plan he dreamed about during the long nights since his return to the Cities. He would hang out his shingle in Jesse, drum Coswell the Quack into retirement, marry Sarah, give her a dozen babies, and live happily ever after. Only Sarah wasn't there, and he didn't know if she ever would be there for him.

"It's not that easy," he whispered, looking down at his sneakers, his voice smoky with emotion.

Julia gave him a long look of empathy and said, "Nothing worth having ever is."

Sarah sat on her bed, staring at her suitcase. Her trip to Ohio had been postponed because of Jacob's illness, but her brother was back to his sweet, mischievous self now and she was to board the noon bus.

She wasn't going to go through with it. Day and night she had struggled with the conflicting emotions inside her. She had never felt so torn. She hated the thought of losing her family, especially of losing contact with Jacob. But

Jacob was not her son and she couldn't live her life only halfway because she wanted to cling to him. It wouldn't be healthy for either of them. She loved her family, but remaining in the Amish faith out of duty alone was hypocritical and her other reason for staying—cowardice—was even worse.

All her life she had wanted something different. All her life she had known deep inside that she wasn't Amish, she was just pretending. All that time she had dreamed of other things and not reached out for them because she was afraid to leave the safe haven of her small close-knit community. That was what Ingrid had been asking her when she had wondered aloud if Sarah would really trust her life to Matt. Did she trust him enough to leave her people and give her life to him?

The answer to that was yes. The next question she had no answer for. Did Matt love her enough to teach her about his world and protect her from the worst of it? Did he love her enough to accept what she wanted to give him? Not knowing made her stomach tie up like a pretzel. He had left her. He had gone back to the city. He may have forgotten her already, but she hoped and prayed not, and she was going to find out for a fact.

The bedroom door opened, and Anna stepped in. She had a beautiful quilt of purple and black folded over her arms like a giant muff. "You are ready to leave then?"

Sarah looked up at her with eyes that begged understanding. "I'm not going to Ohio, Mom."

"I know," Anna murmured with a sad smile, tears sparkling like stars in her eyes. "I've always known you wouldn't stay with us, Sarah. You belong to another world in your head and in your heart you belong with your English doctor."

"Please don't hate me for it," Sarah said. "It can't be wrong. I love him too much."

"I couldn't hate you, *bussli*. You were all along meant to leave us. *Es waar Gotters Wille*."

"Oh, Mom," Sarah whispered through her tears. She rose from the bed and hugged her mother, quilt and all.

"I brought this for you," Anna said, sniffling, trying bravely to smile as she held the quilt out when Sarah stepped back from her.

Sarah ran her hand over the fine patchwork of broadcloth. It was an Amish tradition for a mother to give her daughter a quilt when the daughter left home to marry. Sarah still had the one her mother had given her when she had married Samuel. It was a labor of love and duty, as was much of Amish life. It was a good life, a simple life, but it wasn't the life meant for her.

"It's beautiful, Mom," she whispered, wishing this parting didn't have to be so painful or so permanent.

"For your new life," Anna said. "Be happy, Sarah, and know that in my heart you will always be my daughter."

Matt slowed his Jag as Jesse came into sight, and he rolled up behind an Amish buggy being pulled by a fractious-looking black horse. The car behind him honked impatiently, and Matt stuck his arm out the window to give the driver the one-finger salute. The moron. Didn't he know this was a part of the country where no one had any business being in a hurry?

The buggy turned off at the welding shop, but a tour bus had stalled in the middle of the street and there was no way around it. Matt sat listening to a Righteous Brothers tape, replaying his plan in his head. He would go to Ingrid first. There was a good chance her grapevine would know the name of the relatives Sarah had been sent to. Then he would beat a path south and do whatever he had to do to convince Sarah she belonged with him in his world more than she belonged in theirs.

His gaze wandered over the herd of tourists that had spilled out of the bus and were heading across the street toward the small depot and gift shop. Another small knot of people stood in the sunshine at the side of the little putty-colored clapboard building, apparently waiting to board a bus bound for some distant place—two elderly women, a bean pole youth with a buzz-cut and army fatigues, and a young Amish woman.

Matt's hands tightened on the steering wheel and he stared hard out his window. His heart pounded like thunder in his chest. Sarah. But how could it be? She was in Ohio. He stared until his eyes hurt, but he just couldn't tell. She was too far away and too well disguised by her black bonnet and heavy cape. He couldn't quite see her face, but something inside him told him it was Sarah, the missing part of his heart and soul.

There was no hope of turning across the street; the traffic was too heavy coming from the other direction. So he simply left his precious gold XJ6 sitting behind the stalled bus.

"Sarah!" he called, glancing from her to the traffic and back. "Sarah, wait! Don't go!"

Sarah felt as if a bolt of lightning had just shot through her. Matt. As the bus for Minneapolis wheeled into place to take her to him, he stood across the street. He had come back. He had come back for her!

"Matt!" She yanked her heavy bonnet off and waved it wildly, laughing with pure joy.

He darted across the street, just managing to escape a brush with the fender of a pickup. He didn't even hear the blast of the horn. He was too intent on Sarah to care about anything else. She hadn't left yet. There was still time. He wasn't sure he could talk her into marrying him in the few minutes before her bus pulled out, but he dredged up a little of his doctor's arrogance and told himself he probably could. He'd gotten her to fall in love with him almost that fast, hadn't he? And if he didn't succeed before the bus left, he would get on the blasted thing and hound her all the way to Ohio. She would end up marrying him if for no other reason than to get a moment's peace.

"Matt, you donkey, you could have been hit by that truck!" she scolded as he rushed up to her. He was breathing hard, and the wind tossed his dark hair in that way she had read of as rakish. He looked more handsome to her than ever, strong and vital and male, his dark eyes glowing, the wind painting color across his high cheekbones. He stopped before her and planted his hands at the waist of his jeans.

"No problem," he said, grinning. "I'm a physician. I can heal myself."

Sarah's mouth curved into her Mona Lisa smile. "You would think so."

He sobered as he drank in the sight of her face. "I did think so until I found out there wasn't a damn thing I could do to fix my broken heart. I came down here to look for a specialist I know, someone who helped me heal once before. But I thought I was going to have to go all the way to Ohio to find her."

"Oh, Matt," she whispered, tingling all over with love. "You really did come back for me?"

"I had to. I found out I couldn't live without you. I didn't want to." He glanced away, taking a deep breath and gathering courage, then his eyes found hers again. "I know what it would cost you to marry me, Sarah. I don't feel like I have the right to ask you, but I'm going to. I know what your family means to you, but I'll give you a family. I'll give you all the family you want. And I'll give you the chance to learn and to be anything you ever dreamed of being. I love you so much, Sarah Troyer," he said, his dark eyes filling. "I thought I loved you enough to let you go, but I love you more than that. I love you so much I want to see you grow and flourish."

Sarah tried to swallow down the knot of emotion in her throat and smile. "I guess I could grow some," she said, teasing. "Seeing as how I'll be needing new clothes anyway."

Matt didn't laugh. There was still too much hanging in the balance for joking. He wanted to believe she was saying she wanted him, but he needed to hear the actual words. "Do you mean it, Sarah? Are you willing to give up everything you have to be with me?"

She reached up and brushed her fingertips against the scar on his chin, her eyes soft and shining with love. "I have nothing without you."

"Then why were you leaving?" Matt asked, his voice straining against the pain of the question.

"I wasn't leaving. I was coming to you. I love you, Matt Thorne. I don't know much about your world except that I want to be in it if you'll have me."

The hydraulics of the big bus beside them hissed, and the doors snapped open like the mouth of some giant beast. Matt glanced up at the destination sign above the windshield. Minneapolis. All the tension drained out of him in a rush, leaving him feeling weak and dizzy. He threw his head back and let out a whoop of joy that turned heads all up and down Jesse's Main Street. The life force that seemed to have been missing from him for the last week surged inside him once again.

He grabbed Sarah against him and twirled her around, delighting in her squeals of surprise and embarrassment. As he set her down, he drove his fingers into her hair, sending hairpins shooting, setting free the thick mass of brown silk that fell in waves to her hips. He bent his head to kiss her, drinking in the taste of her as if she were the finest, sweetest wine, and she wound her arms around his neck and melted against him.

"Hey!" the bus driver called out the door. "Are you getting on or not?"

"No," Matt said. He waved the bus on, never taking his eyes off the small, pretty woman who would bask in the glow of his love for the rest of his life, who would give him joy and children and make his world bright and new.

"Go on without us," he said. "We're already home."

About the Author

TAMI HOAG's novels have appeared regularly on national bestseller lists since the publication of her first book in 1988. She lives in Virginia with her husband and a menagerie of pets.